THE BIG CRUNCH

THE BIG CRUNCH

PETE HAUTMAN

SCHOLASTIC PRESS · NEW YORK

All rights reserved. Published by Scholastic
Press, an imprint of Scholastic Inc., *Publishers
since 1920*. SCHOLASTIC, SCHOLASTIC PRESS,
and associated logos are trademarks and/or
registered trademarks of Scholastic Inc.

Library of Congress Cataloging-in-Publication
Data Available

ISBN 978-0-545-24075-8

10 9 8 7 6 5 4 3 2 1   11 12 13 14 15 16

Printed in the U.S.A.   23

First edition, January 2011

The text was set in Adobe Caslon Pro with
Trade Gothic Bold Condensed No. 20.
Book design by Christopher Stengel

For Mary, yet again.

FALL

CHAPTER ONE

THE FIRST TIME WES SAW JUNE, he thought she was kind of funny-looking. She had these thick lips, a wide mouth, greenish-blue eyes that were a little too far apart, and her hair — a dark blond color — looked still wet from her morning shower. Wes thought she looked like a sea creature pretending to be human.

But that was the first time, language arts, the first class of the day on the first day of junior year, a quick look three rows over as he was checking out everybody, not just the girls. He knew maybe half of them. Most of the rest looked halfway familiar. It was a big school.

Later, remembering that moment, he seemed to recall that there was something else about her — an aura of hot maple syrup and fresh-turned soil — but he figured that was all in his head.

That first day in English — what this school called "language arts" — June did not notice Wes. She was too busy having the worst morning of her life, due to having a stupid argument with her insane mother on the way out the door, spilling cranberry juice on her jeans when the bus hit a pothole, and getting her hair crapped on by a pigeon as she walked into school. Also, she was ninety-nine percent certain that she would get her period before the end of the day and she'd forgotten to bring anything and she didn't know one single person she could borrow from and there were no tampon machines anywhere. She was already starting to hate Minnesota.

Her second class, studio arts, was a little better. Her hair finally dried from the emergency wash job in the girls' restroom, and she made a friend, a chatty girl named Naomi. It was enough to get her through the second hour of the day. And, it turned out, Naomi was the sort of girl who was never without an extra tampon.

At lunch that day, Wes's eyes once again landed on the fish girl. She was sitting with Naomi Liddell. Wes felt the sort of smug pity that comes with seeing someone else in dire straits.

Naomi Liddell had a history of glomming on to anyone who would so much as smile at her — it didn't matter who. She would then proceed to inflict her grating, incessant monotone on her new victim. No one stayed friends with Naomi for long. The new girl already had that glazed look of one whose brain cells were rapidly turning to tapioca. Her hair looked better, though — not so flat and wet-looking, and lighter in color, and her eyes had this aqua tint that made him think of swimming pools. He decided to think of her as Aqua Girl, which was much nicer than Fish Girl.

June quickly figured out that sitting with Naomi was like having LOSER tattooed across her forehead. She imagined escape strategies ranging from faking an epileptic fit to plugging Naomi's yak hole with a wadded-up napkin. June's eyes drifted around the lunchroom as Naomi catalogued what various girls — none of whom June knew or cared about — had worn to school last year. Or maybe it was the year before. Or maybe she was reciting the J. Crew catalog.

As Naomi continued to attack her left eardrum, June thought about how every school she had been to — six of them in the past four years — was pretty much the same. Her father's business required frequent relocations. June had learned how to recognize which kids were cool but not too cool, and which ones were the users, posers, geeks, skanks, preps, gangstas, macho-morons, punks, burnouts, and so forth. It wasn't that complicated. The best-dressed girls were generally backstabbers, the best-looking guy was always full of himself, and the scariest, most tatted, most studded, most black-leathery person in school was inevitably shy and gentle and, once you got past the studs and skulls, not actually all that interesting.

Most importantly, she had learned early on that anybody eager to make her acquaintance the first day was almost certainly desperate for a friend, and therefore undesirable as such. There was always a Naomi, another barnacle clamping on, another harpoon, another anchor to drag . . . and the worst thing was that even if June stood up right then and screamed *"Bitch!"* right in Naomi's face, the connection would still be there. She would always know that Naomi was out there, and would be clanking along behind her for the rest of her life and beyond. June knew why house-haunting ghosts dragged chains — those were the connections they'd made with the living.

Wes, who classified himself as a semi-cool semi-geek, could have told June who was who and what was what in about five minutes, but at that time he was on the other side of the lunchroom catching up with the two Alans — Schwartz and Hurd. Alan Hurd had spent the summer working at his uncle's resort up on Otter Tail

Lake, where he was in charge of cleaning fish, among other things. He claimed to be able to fillet a walleye in twelve seconds. He also claimed to have hooked up "every way you can think of" with a hot nineteen-year-old who worked at the resort doing child care and water aerobics classes.

The other Alan, Alan Schwartz, confessed that the only action he'd seen all summer was a copy of *Penthouse* he'd grabbed out of his next-door neighbor's recycling.

"How come you were digging through your neighbor's garbage?" Alan Hurd asked.

"There was no excavation involved. It was recycling, not garbage." Alan Schwartz shoved an entire mini-taco into his maxi-mouth.

Wes said, "How come you didn't just go online for your porn?"

Alan Schwartz scrunched up his face and swallowed. "My dad put all this spy crap on my computer after he got that one bill."

Alan Hurd laughed. "Sex is way better in the flesh."

"In your dreams," said Alan Schwartz.

They both looked at Wes, as if he could render judgment.

Wes said, "I broke up with Izzy."

Alan Schwartz inserted a second mini-taco into his mouth and said, as he chewed, "Are you out of your freaking mind?"

Fortunately, June had just one class — and lunch period — with Naomi Liddell. After lunch was trigonometry. She'd signed up for that because she already knew trig from her last school, so she could count on at least one easy A. She sat on the window side toward the back to get a look at the other students. Mostly boys. Mostly disappointing.

June knew that she would probably be moving to some other school next year, if not before, so she didn't have a lot of time to establish herself here. The important thing was to find a group of girls she could hang with, and a guy. The two things were related. For example, if she joined the book club — there was always a book club — and hung out with them, her choice of guys would be limited to the dark and moody Chuck Palahniuk/Kurt Vonnegut/Life-Sucks-and-Then-You-Die brooders. If she took up with the high-fashion crowd, she'd end up with some guy with a thumb ring, always playing with his hair and agonizing over the length of his jeans. And if she tried out for cheerleader like she'd done at the school before last, she'd end up going to prom with some jock. Which was not necessarily bad, but she didn't want to spend every Friday night in October sitting on cold aluminum bleachers watching boys channel their inner Neanderthals.

What she hoped for was a guy who was reasonably intelligent but not too geeky or obsessive. A guy who smelled okay and had a sense of humor. In short, somebody she could have fun with, but not miss too much when her folks pulled up stakes and moved her to Butthole, Missouri, or Armpit, Tennessee. She considered joining the drama club. Naturally, the male wannabe actors would all be gay, ADD, clinically insane, or all three, but she might hook up with someone on the stage crew. She'd once had a boyfriend who did lighting, and he'd been okay if you didn't mind the nail biting and the nervous laughter. At least he'd known how to fix stuff.

As June was having these thoughts, another part of herself looked on with arms crossed and a knowing smile.

So you're just a boy shopper looking for a love stud, said Sarcastic June.

There were several alternate Junes: Sarcastic June, Scornful June, Guilty June, and Fearful June. She also had Pragmatic June, who could say, *I did not choose to be here. I just want to have some fun, and get through the day, and move on.*

You have no true feelings, said Scornful June. *You are hollow inside.*

"I do too feel," June whispered.

Like you would even know what real feelings are, said Sarcastic June.

June feared that Sarcastic June was right. Her feelings lacked depth. She knew that some people experienced feelings of such power and intensity that they could do anything — climb a mountain, commit hara-kiri, sacrifice a loved one — anything. June could not imagine herself doing anything like that. Her emotions lay upon her like a thin, moist film, easily evaporated, never present in quantity.

You're a robot, said Scornful June. *You go through the motions without caring about why.*

There is no why, said Pragmatic June.

Like you would know, said Sarcastic June.

"I have no soul," said June.

"What?" said a voice in her ear.

June turned her head to look at the boy sitting next to her. He had a broad face, glasses with gold frames, and short dark hair combed straight forward in raggedy bangs.

"Excuse me?" said June.

"You said something," said the boy.

"No, I didn't."

The boy shrugged. "I thought I heard you say something."

"I was just clearing my throat."

"It sounded like you said, 'I have no soap.'"

"Ahem!" The teacher, Mr. Hallstrom, was glaring at them. "I hate to interrupt, but we have a class going on here, and we would all appreciate it if you two lovebirds would shut up and listen."

The boy's cheeks turned instantly red.

June said, simply, "Sorry."

Mr. Hallstrom harrumphed, then went back to talking about how to measure the height of a tree based on the length of its shadow and other trig stuff June already knew. She sneaked a look at the boy next to her. He was taking notes, pressing his pen hard against his notebook, his blush still in evidence. June never blushed — more evidence that she had the emotional depth of a gnat, according to Sarcastic June. This boy obviously had strong emotions. She imagined herself riding in a car with him. Would he have a car? He didn't look like a boy who would have his own car.

Later, in the hallway, at her locker, he came up to her and said, "Sorry I got you in trouble back there."

"It's okay," June replied.

He held out his hand. "Jerry Preuss, future class president."

June wasn't sure which was dorkier — the handshake offer or the "class president" bit. She didn't know what else to do, so she shook his hand.

"I'm June Edberg."

"June — like the month?"

"It's kind of an old-fashioned name," June said. "I'm lucky they didn't name me February."

It was a dumb joke she'd used a hundred times before. Jerry gave her a blank look for a second, then he got it and laughed.

"Did you just move here?" he asked.

"A few weeks ago. I used to live in Chicago."

"My cousin lives in Chicago."

June smiled but didn't say anything.

After a few seconds, she could see the red returning to his cheeks, and felt sorry for him.

"Are you really running for class president?"

"Yeah. I'm just starting to campaign."

June held back a laugh. "That's pretty ambitious."

"I know. So . . . what would it take to get your vote?"

"Five bucks."

It took him a couple of beats to see she was kidding, and then he was embarrassed for not getting it right away. "Seriously," he said.

"Seriously?"

"I'm trying to figure out how to get people to vote for me."

"Don't most politicians just promise people whatever they want?" She laughed — it sounded totally phony. "How about a four-day school week?"

Jerry Preuss's soft brown eyes glistened. He nodded vigorously, as if she'd said something insanely brilliant, and shifted his feet to bring him a few inches closer, so close she could see the pores on his nose.

"That's good!" he said. "Anything else?"

June, her back pressed against her locker, wanted to scream.

"I gotta go," she said. "Good luck with your campaign." She slipped past him and walked quickly off down the hall.

It was not that she was afraid of him. Jerry wasn't repulsive or anything. He seemed like a nice guy. But she sensed yet another manacle about to clamp on to her. Another dragging chain. Another attachment she would eventually have to tear away.

Every time, it hurt.

THE FIRST TIME WES HEARD JUNE EDBERG'S NAME, he didn't connect it with Aqua Girl.

"There's this girl June, in my trig class? She talks to herself," Jerry Preuss said. Jerry was Wes's oldest friend.

"What does she say?" Wes asked.

" 'I have no soap.' "

"What does that mean?"

"She's from Chicago."

"They don't have soap in Chicago?"

They were standing outside where the buses were loading, waiting until the last minute to get on. The less time spent in a school bus the better.

"I need a car," Jerry said.

"Everybody needs a car."

"I need money to get a car. My parents won't buy me one."

"Join the club." Wes needed a car too, but his summer job at the nursery had only netted him nine hundred dollars after expenses, and a lot of that he'd spent on junk. What was left was hardly enough for gas and insurance. He'd been thinking about getting a used scooter. If he could talk his mom into it.

"How come you broke up with Izzy?" Jerry asked.

"She was being too needy." It was a lie. Izzy was one of the least needy people he'd ever known. He didn't actually know why they'd broken up. It wasn't as if they'd had a fight, or even stopped liking each other. He'd just gotten . . . *tired*. It was exhausting, knowing Isabel O'Connor was always there, knowing his phone could ring at any moment and it would be her, and knowing that anything he did would be a thing she would have to think was okay or else it would become this thing he had to hide and feel guilty about, and knowing that all his friends thought of him not as Wes, but as Wes-and-Iz, Iz-and-Wes, and most of all knowing that she existed, that she was out there thinking about him. Everything he did and everything she did was tied together in a big snarly knot with a thousand invisible strands.

He had tried talking to Izzy about it once, the invisible strand thing, but she started laughing so he shut up about it. It was just a way to think about things.

"Besides," he said to Jerry, "I don't really want a girlfriend at this stage of my life."

"What stage is that?" Jerry asked.

Wes shrugged. "You know. Junior year."

The weird thing was that breaking up had been Wes's idea, and it had taken him *weeks* to build up the courage to break it to her, and then when he told Izzy, she'd been like, *Yeah, whatever, cool.* He was immediately sure that if he hadn't suggested the breakup, she would have, so the feeling of freedom he'd been looking forward to turned into a sick feeling, like *Now what?* Now that he didn't have Izzy anymore, some supposedly useless little part of him had left a hole that was filling up with this stuff, a little bag of grit sitting in his gut. So instead of invisible strands he had a sack of dirt riding on his liver.

"Wes!" Jerry was suddenly twenty feet away, standing at the bus door. "You getting on?"

Wes looked at the long, yellow-orange bus, at the blurry faces behind the dirty windows, and suddenly he had this flash that if he got on, everybody on the bus would attach to him with a new invisible strand. A fly caught in a spiderweb.

"I'm gonna walk," he said.

Jerry shrugged and climbed aboard. The bus doors closed.

June's parents had rented a house eleven blocks away from Wellstone High. Her mother had presented this information to her as if it were a gift.

"I know you hated that long bus ride in Schaumburg, so we found this place close to your new school."

June knew that her convenience had nothing to do with why her parents had chosen this house. The fact that it was near school was purely coincidental, but her mother, typically, had taken credit for supposedly making sacrifices to enhance her poor, pathetic daughter's life.

"You can walk to school in five minutes," her mother had said.

More like ten, June thought. "What about in winter? When it's, like, twenty below? I'll freeze."

"It doesn't get *that* cold here."

"We're in Minnesota, aren't we? Icebox of the nation?" Not that what she said could have changed anything.

She had timed herself on the way to school that morning. Eleven minutes, thirty-four seconds. If they were still living here in January — no sure thing — eleven minutes, thirty-four seconds was enough time to book a serious frostbite.

She decided to time herself again on the way home. Maybe she could cut her time down to ten minutes if she walked faster and cut a few corners.

Unfortunately, Naomi Liddell latched on to her as she was leaving the school and yakked her ears raw with something about the school paper. June didn't know what Naomi was going on about, except that she seemed intent on getting June involved in some sort of after-school activity involving sticking address labels on envelopes. June finally extricated herself by saying she had a dentist appointment, which she didn't.

"Which dentist do you see?" Naomi asked.

"Um, I don't know." That was the problem with lies. They got complicated. "My mom made the appointment."

"I bet it's Posnick. He's nice."

"I'll let you know," June said, edging away. She checked the time on her cell phone. "I gotta go." She started walking fast.

"See you tomorrow!" Naomi called after her.

June put Naomi out of her mind and gave herself to the rhythm of her heels scuffing the sidewalk. About halfway home she saw a boy ahead of her going in the same direction but walking much more slowly. As she drew closer she noticed his hair — pale brown, kind of on the long side — and his shirt — plaid, unbuttoned, tails flapping in the light breeze. Faded black jeans. Dirty white basketball shoes. He was shuffling along, in no hurry, but every few steps he would sort of skip, or maybe he was kicking something.

He was kicking a rock, moving it down the sidewalk in front of him.

June slowed down when she got about twenty paces behind

him. She didn't want to startle him and throw him off his rhythm. He had probably been kicking that same rock for blocks.

On the other hand, she was making good time, and she hated that this guy was holding her up. She sped up her pace and walked past him, staying out of the way of the rock by walking on the grassy strip between the sidewalk and the street. As they came next to each other, she glanced over at him and their eyes met. He kicked the rock too hard; it bounced up onto somebody's lawn. June gave him a flat smile and kept walking, but the image of his face stayed with her, those startled brown eyes, that open mouth. He reminded her of other boys she'd met, but there was also something different. Something about those eyes, the way he looked at her.

Aqua Girl walked really fast. Wes tried to match her speed, but he couldn't do it without sort of half running. He gave up after a few seconds; the gap between them widened.

He kept following her even after passing Fourteenth Street, the street that led, after another mile of nearly identical houses, to the nearly identical house where he lived.

The girl kept up her rapid pace for several blocks, then turned a corner.

Wes, a block behind her, sped up until he was almost to the corner, then returned to his nonchalant shuffle. He stopped at the corner. She was nowhere in sight. She must live in one of the houses near the corner. Not that it mattered. He didn't even know why he'd followed her. Just something to do. Stupid. He'd added half a mile to his long walk home.

He thought about taking the shortcut across Jenkins Park, then decided against it. Izzy lived right on the park. It would be too weird to run into her.

For nearly eighteen months — an eternity — Izzy O'Connor and Wes Andrews had been monogamous, a constant part of each other's life. They had talked two or three times every day. Wes had been a regular dinner guest at the O'Connors'. He called Izzy's mom Mrs. O'C, and he called her dad by his nickname, Hap.

Izzy had spent plenty of time at Wes's house too, most often when Wes was drafted into babysitting his sister, Paula, who had recently turned ten and declared herself too old to need a sitter.

He had only seen Izzy once at school that first day, sitting in the lunchroom with her artsy friends. They were laughing and making things out of straws. That was the sort of thing she liked to do. Always bending and twisting and coloring things to make them look like other things.

People were always saying what a pretty girl Izzy was, and it was true. Though over the past year her face had become so much a part of Wes's life that seeing her was almost like seeing his own face in a mirror. Except that at lunch that day — the first time he'd seen her since they'd broken up two weeks ago — her hair had been shorter.

At Sixteenth Street, Wes caught a whiff of something baking. Something sweet. He turned left and followed his nose to the Bun & Brew.

The Bun & Brew — "brew" as in coffee, not beer — had taken over an old filling station, still with the antique pumps out front, forty-nine cents a gallon for regular. They didn't work, of course.

Inside, the nostalgia theme intensified: photos of old cars, Formica tabletops, and a working eight-track tape deck constantly playing oldies so moldy they were actually semi-cool. The tables were set up in the old garage bay; the office had been converted into an espresso bar and baked-goods case. A muffin would kill the stomach clench, and it wouldn't take his every last dime. He shuffled up to the counter. Eight types of muffins, three varieties of croissant, a killer chocolate éclair, and some giant chocolate chip cookies. He always ordered the blueberry muffin.

"Can I help you?"

Wes looked up. On the other side of the counter stood Izzy, her face carefully arranged in that tight half smile she used with complete strangers.

His heart did a *ka-thunk*.

"Iz . . . you work here now?"

Izzy nodded, still holding the smile.

"Cool," said Wes. A really stupid thing to say because it was not cool at all, her working there, where if he wanted a blueberry muffin, he would have to see her all the time.

"Blueberry muffin?" she asked.

"Cookie," he said, not wanting to be too predictable.

Izzy grabbed a tissue and got him a cookie.

"How's Paulalicious?" she asked. That was her nickname for his sister. Izzy had a nickname for everybody. She'd come up with some really weird ones for him. Like Pookie.

"She thinks she's an adult already. Two digits."

"Oh, right — her tenth birthday. Tell her happy birthday for me."

"Okay." Wes knew he wouldn't. Paula was still mad at him for breaking up with Izzy, who she worshipped. He paid for his cookie and stood awkwardly as she counted out his change and handed it to him. She smiled, a real smile this time. Wes felt a smile begin to form on his own face, then realized she was looking over his shoulder. A woman stood behind him, waiting to place her order. Wes stepped aside and carried his cookie to a table, sat down, watched Izzy ring up a coffee and a muffin, stood up, took his cookie outside, and ate it as he walked home.

He didn't even really like cookies.

CHAPTER
THREE

SHE WASN'T SUPPOSED TO CALL SCHAUMBURG, or any of the other places they'd lived before. Her parents were fanatical about that.

"Move on, Junie," her mom had said. "The past is the past."

" 'There Is No Reverse Gear in Time Machine,' " her father said, quoting the title of a book he'd once read.

"But isn't the whole point of a time machine so you can go back?" June said.

"Not *this* time machine. This time machine only goes forward, into the future. *Next!*" Like a counterman in a deli, he loved to yell, *Next!*

Her mother said, "Junie, you'll probably never see any of those kids again. Best to make a clean break."

"Why?" June asked.

"Junie, I know it's hard moving from one school to another. But hanging on to the past is not the way to deal with it."

"Why?" she asked again.

"Please don't be difficult," her mother said.

June scrolled through the numbers on her cell, remembering faces to go with the names. Brent. Gerry. Felicity. Heather. Katie. Kevin. Krista D. Krista K. So many *K* names. LeBron. Octavia. Prathi . . .

June knew her mother was right. The past was gone forever. Nobody in Schaumburg probably even thought about her anymore. Or if they did, it was like, *Remember that girl? The one with blond hair?*

You mean Teresa?

No. The one that moved a few weeks ago, you know. The one who was going out with Brent?

Oh yeah, um, I'm pretty sure her name started with a "J."

Jennie? Jenna?

Something like that.

"June."

June looked up. Her mother, carrying two bags of groceries, was standing in the doorway.

"What are you doing?"

"Sitting at the kitchen table."

"Well, put down your phone and help me with these groceries."

Later that night, June picked up her phone and once again looked at her contact list. It was blank. All the numbers had disappeared, erased, gone forever.

Wes's mom and his little sister were in the kitchen having one of their arguments when Wes got home. Neither of them noticed him. Paula was being a brat, as usual, and Mom was falling all over herself trying to please her.

"Honey pie, I am not going to buy you a new pair of shoes just because Lynette Stiles told you your shoes were stupid. She's only being mean."

"Nobody wears Skechers anymore."

"Honey, that's not true. Lots of kids your age *love* Skechers."

"Yeah, the dweebs and morons."

"You liked them fine when we bought them. Does that make you a dweeb?"

"If you make me *wear* them, yeah."

"Don't you think that Lynette was just trying to make you feel bad?"

"The *shoes* are bad."

"And suppose you wear new shoes to school tomorrow, will that make Lynette think you're cool?"

"I don't care what she thinks."

"I'll tell you what she'll think — she'll think she has power over you. She might say your jeans are dorky. What then?"

"My jeans aren't dorky. These shoes are."

"Honey, don't you think . . ."

Wes grabbed a bottle of juice from the fridge and took it out to the garage, where he wouldn't have to listen. He knew how it would end. Paula would be in tears and locked in her bedroom, and his mom would come looking for him and saddle him with some heinous task — mowing the yard, or sorting his dirty laundry — just to remind herself that she could still control her children. She wouldn't cave to Paula's demand for new shoes, but she would probably take her to the mall and buy her a new belt or something.

The garage was a refuge of sorts. It contained several half-finished repair projects: his dad's prehistoric ten-speed with the bent wheel, an outboard engine with a broken prop and no boat, a rocking chair that needed a new armrest, and so forth. One corner was filled with Wes's skateboard collection and other sports gear. There was a table saw, a drill press, and assorted other tools, and several lawn care items: weed whacker, leaf blower, push mower, trimmer, edger, spreader. There was no room for their two cars. That was one of his mom's pet peeves. About once a year she would throw a fit, and Wes and his dad would rearrange and clean and get rid of a few things — just enough to fit Mom's car inside. And then they would start accumulating again, buying things like the infamous and enormous commercial sod cutter, which his dad had picked up dirt cheap at an auction. The sod cutter had sat in the garage for two years, never used, until one day Wes's mom wheeled it out to the curb — she must have been really mad, that thing was *heavy* — and put a FREE sign on it. An hour later, it was gone.

Wes's dad couldn't believe she'd given away his sod cutter.

"When were you ever going to cut sod?" his mom had said.

"It was worth a lot of money, Rita."

"So why didn't you sell it?"

"I was going to get around to it."

"Well, I've saved you the trouble."

Wes turned on the light over the cluttered eight-foot-long workbench and sat on one of the three ancient leather-covered bar stools from the Hotel LaGrange, which had been torn down before Wes was born.

"Why do you need three stools?" his mother had once asked. "There are never more than two of you out here."

"The stools are cool," Wes had said. His dad had backed him up. That was one argument they'd won. Something Wes had figured out — learned from Izzy and her artist parents, actually — was that purely aesthetic judgments were unassail-able. If you said you liked something, or loved it — like when Iz declared that vintage blue jeans were the most beautiful garment ever created — people could disagree all they wanted but never be able to prove you wrong. Of course, to make it work, you had to not care what anybody else thought, and you had to believe.

Wes believed in the stools.

Wes looked around the garage, hoping he might be inspired to do something. The workbench alone made him want to curl up and scream. He couldn't even see the top of it. What *was* all this? Scraps of used sandpaper. Bent nails. Worn-out drill bits and Allen wrenches and pieces of electrical cord and a busted desk lamp and a pile of rusty upholstery tacks and a squeeze bottle of Elmer's glue, open on its side and permanently cemented to a box of dry-wall screws. The bench was both an archaeological wonder and testament to the utter and undeniable incapacity of father and son to clean up after themselves.

Overcome with a wave of revulsion and shame, Wes got up, kicked the stools aside, and tipped the workbench onto the floor.

Two hours later, Wes's father got home from work and looked into the garage to find his son sitting on the floor sorting screws and nails and upholstery tacks into small piles.

"Wes, what the hell?" he said.

"Hi, Dad."

Mr. Andrews noticed that the top of the workbench was com-pletely empty, and that it had been painted green.

"You painted the workbench green?" he said.

"I like green," said Wes. "Green is cool."

"Oh. What color was it?"

"White, I think."

"What got into you?"

"It's kind of hard to explain," said Wes.

By the end of her first week at Wellstone, June had made three new friends — Jess, Britt, and Phoebe. Jessica Weitz was a tall, thin girl with flawless-but-quirky fashion instincts, Britt Spinoza had her own car, and Phoebe Keller's brother worked at First Avenue, the famous Minneapolis nightclub. June was accepted into their circle by virtue of her cosmopolitan background — she told them she'd lived in Chicago, Kansas City, Phoenix, Dallas, and a few other places all bigger and more exciting than here. June did not mention that most of her homes had not technically been in the cities she cited, but in the stunningly boring suburbs preferred by her parents.

Naomi Liddell attempted to use June to inveigle herself into the group, but was met with the sort of icy politeness that even she was unable to overlook. June felt bad about shrugging off Naomi, but her relief outweighed her guilt.

Jess, Britt, and Phoebe had several male friends they occasionally dated, though as near as June could tell, none of the girls had a boyfriend in the usual sense.

"Our job is to have fun," Phoebe declared one afternoon as they were drinking iced coffees at the Bun & Brew. "I need a boyfriend like I need a third boob."

Jess gave Phoebe a look and jerked her head toward the counter behind them, where a girl with short dark hair was taking an order from a sour-faced old man wearing a leather cap with earflaps.

"Just coffee," the man said. "No capu-whatever, no flavors, no milk, no nothing. Just a cup of coffee."

"Dark roast, breakfast blend, or decaf?" the girl asked.

"Surprise me," the man snapped.

"Decaf it is," said the girl.

Jess leaned over the table and lowered her voice. "You heard Izzy and Wes broke up?"

Who's Izzy? June wondered. *Who's Wes?*

"So?" said Phoebe.

"So it seems kind of, I don't know, rude. To be talking about boyfriends with her standing right over there."

"She can't hear us. Besides, I wasn't talking about her."

"Wes and Izzy were practically married," Britt said.

"That's Izzy behind the counter?" June asked.

Britt nodded.

"Who's Wes?"

"You've seen him, I'm sure."

"He's in our English class," said Phoebe.

"You mean language arts?"

"Yeah, English. Floppy hair? Kind of cute?"

June knew right away who she meant.

Wes had almost gotten used to seeing Izzy at school. It helped that she had shorter hair now, and some clothes he hadn't seen, almost as if she had become a different person. He was also getting used to not having one special person to talk to about everything all the time. The closest thing he had was Jerry Preuss. Not that they had much in common anymore. Jerry had decided to become Emperor of the Universe or something, and he was kicking off his political career by running for class president. Wes cared less about who was class president than he did about, well, anything. He didn't even know who the current class president was, so it was awkward when, during a study period at the library, Jerry asked him to work on his campaign.

"The main thing is to create buzz," Jerry told him.

"Bzzzzz," said Wes.

Jerry didn't laugh. "Seriously. I need you to talk me up."

"To who?"

"Everybody."

"You want me to go around saying nice things about you all day?"

"Not *all* day. Just whenever you get a chance. Remind people about the election, and mention my qualifications."

"What qualifications?"

"I'd be proactive. I'd get things done. I'd —"

"Get what things done?"

"Whatever the student body wants."

"Free pizza? Optional homework?"

"Anything within reason."

"Do you know you've suddenly gotten incredibly boring?"

"Thanks a lot!"

"If you're going to run for office, you'd better learn to handle criticism." Wes could hear his father's voice coming out of his own mouth.

"Not from my friends."

"*Especially* from your friends."

Jerry looked so stricken that Wes took pity on him and promised to create buzz. Tons of buzz. He would turn Wellstone into a giant beehive of pro-Jerry buzz.

"Thank you," said Jerry.

Later that day, Wes ran into Izzy — almost literally ran into her as he came rushing around a corner.

"Hey, Wes," she said, giving him the same cautious smile she'd given him at the Bun & Brew.

"Uh. Hi."

"Where are you headed?"

"Chemistry. You?"

"English. So what's new?"

"Uh . . . Jerry Preuss for class president?"

Izzy laughed. "You're such a goof!" She walked around him and headed for her class.

Wes stared after her. It was almost like old times, her calling him a goof, and it made him think that maybe some of the good feelings he and Izzy had shared were still there. So breaking up wasn't that bad.

After school, once again waiting until the last second to board the bus, Wes told Jerry that he had been creating big-time buzz.

"How?" Jerry asked.

"I am inserting your name into every conversation. I even brought it up in science."

"How did you do that?"

"We were doing acids and bases and using litmus paper to tell the difference. I asked Reinhardt what politicians mean when they talk about litmus tests, and —"

"When do politicians talk about litmus paper?"

"Litmus *tests*. Like when the president says, 'I will not use a litmus test for selecting the next Supreme Court judge!' "

"What does that mean?"

"I'm not exactly sure," Wes admitted. "But they say it all the time." He was beginning to think he knew more about politics than Jerry.

"What did Reinhardt say?"

"He said to ask my American history teacher. I said, 'Maybe I'll ask Jerry Preuss. He knows a lot about government.' "

Jerry thought for a moment. "Did anybody laugh?"

"Nope."

"That's pretty good."

"Bzzzzz."

"We'd better get on."

Wes looked at the bus. "I think I'm gonna walk," he said.

FIVE

JUNE ONCE AGAIN FOUND HERSELF catching up with the floppy-haired guy from her language arts class. Only this time he wasn't kicking a rock, he was just sort of shambling along with his hands in his pockets, head tipped forward like he was watching the sidewalk. She was sure he was the guy that Jess and Phoebe had been talking about, the one who used to go out with that girl Izzy.

He was walking oddly again, the sort of shuffle with an occasional hop thrown in. June focused on his feet and quickly figured out that he was trying not to step on the cracks. Another guy with a case of arrested development.

June slowed down and followed him at a distance of about fifty feet. Not so close that he would hear her and turn around. They proceeded for about a block that way, two rogue planets following the same path, until the guy suddenly stopped, looked straight down, and bent over to tie his shoe. Either she would have to catch up with him or stop completely. She kept walking. A few seconds later, just as he stood up, she came up alongside him.

He looked at her and jerked back his head, as if he found her somewhat repellent.

June stopped and said, "What?"

"Nothing!" he said. "You just . . . I didn't know you were there."

"It's a public sidewalk, right?"

"Yeah! I didn't mean, uh . . . you're in Ms. Blum's class, right? First period?"

June nodded, watching his face. His brown eyes moved in little jerks from her mouth to her eyes to her hair. His eyebrows were slightly crooked, as if he was on the verge of asking a question.

"My name's Wes," he said.

"I'm June."

"Cool."

Cool? Why would he think her name was *cool?*

"I think I was named after my grandmother," June said. "I'm just glad her name wasn't February."

He laughed, even though she'd kind of screwed up the joke, which wasn't much of a joke to begin with.

"Grandma February," Wes said. "I have a Grandma May, short for Mavis."

"And they didn't name you Mavis?"

"No, but my middle name is August."

They stared at each other. June thought he was kidding, but she wasn't a hundred percent sure.

"You live around here?" he asked after a moment.

June hesitated before responding. Her instinct was to never share personal information unnecessarily, but he had, after all, told her his middle name. She waved her hand in the direction they had been walking.

Wes nodded, as if that was all he wanted to know. "I live on Fourteenth," he said.

There was an awkward moment then when neither of them said anything and they were just standing there on the sidewalk. After about three amazingly long seconds, June said, "Oh,

Fourteenth," which was a pretty lame thing to say, but it was all she could think of at the moment.

The thing that really got Wes was how far apart her eyes were. It made him feel as if she were looking at him from two different directions. Not that they were freakish or anything. And if the average person's eyes were, say, an inch and a quarter apart, June's were maybe an inch and a quarter plus a sixteenth — just the tiniest bit more. They were impossible to not look at — big, almond-shaped, the color of a clean swimming pool on a sunny day. Wes had to make a conscious effort to move his eyes around so she wouldn't think they were in a staring contest. He looked from her wide mouth to her little nose with three freckles to the tiny V-shaped scar on her chin.

Almost at the same moment, even though neither of them had said anything, they both started walking.

Wes said, "You just move here?"

"A few weeks ago," she said. "From Chicago."

"I've never been."

"Schaumburg, actually. It's a suburb."

"I guess suburbs are the same everywhere."

June stopped and turned her head sharply. "What makes you say that?" Her voice had an edge to it; Wes felt the muscles in his neck clench. But when he looked at her, he could see that she wasn't angry.

He said, "It's just that every suburb I've been to is kind of the same."

June stared at him. "That was weird."

"What was?"

"What you said was exactly the same thought, word for word, that went through my head a nanosecond before you said it."

Wes grinned. "I guess I'm psychic."

"Psych-o, maybe." She laughed, letting him know she was kidding. "So what am I thinking right now?"

Wes closed his eyes and waited for an image to appear. "You're thinking about a double bacon cheeseburger," he said after a moment.

"Wrong."

"What were you thinking?"

"I'd rather not say."

"Not fair!"

"Okay, actually, you weren't that far off. I was thinking about a chocolate éclair."

"Both food. High fat. Delicious."

"Exactly. But that could just be because it's teatime."

"You drink tea?"

"No. But sitting down to a mid-afternoon snack and a caffeinated beverage strikes me as a very civilized custom." They had started walking again.

"I agree," said Wes, suddenly acutely aware that he had exactly twenty-six cents in his pocket. They had reached the corner of Twelfth and Hendricks. He stopped and pointed up Twelfth Street. "This is where I get off."

"Oh!" said June, her eyes widening slightly.

"I live about half a mile that way," Wes said.

"I thought you lived on Fourteenth?"

"I take Twelfth down to Barnard, then up to Fourteenth."

"Oh. Well. It was nice talking."

"I'm supposed to be home when my little sister gets there," Wes said. It was not strictly true — Paula was notoriously competent on her own, but he felt the need to give June some reason for leaving, but not the real reason — that if they walked by the B&B, he couldn't afford to buy anything, and if she bought herself that éclair he would just be standing there like a broke-ass idiot. Plus, there was the whole Izzy thing.

"I get it," June said.

Wes pondered those three words all the way home.

June's parents were at some business thing, so she made her own dinner: a cheese and green pepper omelet, a handful of Ritz crackers, and a kosher pickle. She put the food on a blue plate and set it on the table. The yellow and green omelet and the orange crackers and the dull green pickle stared back at her. Suddenly, it did not look like food; it looked like a very bad painting. Her appetite deserted her. She scraped the omelet into the trash, put the crackers back in their box, and returned the pickle to its jar.

Later, she worked her way through a tray of chocolate chip cookies as she flipped through television channels. At one point she paused at an infomercial for Sani-Made, the company that had hired her father as a consultant. Sani-Made had started out as a diaper service, then branched out into other baby products like cribs and toys and pacifiers. In the infomercial, they were selling Gerald Genius, a $49.95 CD set that supposedly would make your baby smarter.

June's father was a workout specialist. It had nothing to do with working out, as in exercising. Elton Edberg was hired by companies that were in trouble. He helped them work their way back to profitability. Most of his jobs only lasted a few months, which was why June had lived so many places.

The infomercial showed an animation of a baby listening happily to his brightly colored Sani-Made CD player, then toddling over to a whiteboard and scrawling out a complex mathematical formula. She could see why the company was in trouble.

The first thing her dad had done when he'd started at Sani-Made was fire half the employees. Then he'd gone into his usual shtick about moving forward, always forward, never looking back, creating a viable future, thinking outside the box, thinking positive, thinking wealthy. He liked to say, "If we can dream it, we can do it!"

June clicked the remote. World War II documentary. *Click.* *Law & Order* rerun. *Click. Leave It to Beaver.* June Cleaver, the perfect 1950s housewife, was making a nutritious meal for Wally and Beaver.

June ate another cookie. *Click.*

One thing Wes hated about himself was that he was always rethinking things he'd said or done, and then figuring how it *should* have gone. It drove him crazy. For example, he kept thinking about talking to that girl, June, and blurting out that he had to go home to babysit his sister. He was sure she had known he was lying. He *should* have said, "The B and B has excellent éclairs."

She would have said, "Let's go!"

And he would have said, "I'm afraid I'm not able to today, as I have other obligations. Perhaps another time?"

That would have been better. Except he didn't really talk like that.

Or, when she had asked him to guess her thoughts, he could have said something besides "double bacon cheeseburger." He could have said, "Molecules." Or, if he'd brought some money with him to school, then he could have offered to buy her an éclair. Better yet, if he hadn't stopped to tie his shoe, then he wouldn't have had to deal with her at all. The last thing he needed was another girlfriend. The whole idea of breaking up with Izzy was to get some freedom. And besides, the reason he hadn't brought any money to school was so that he wouldn't spend it on something stupid like éclairs.

And why had he told her his middle name was *August*? He hoped she got it, that he was kidding.

He was still thinking about all that when he got home, so he went straight to the garage to admire the results of his cleaning project. Over the previous three afternoons he had swept, scrubbed, and organized every part of the garage — even to the point of painting the floor light gray. Wes sat on one of the stools and let himself be soothed by his surroundings. An island of orderliness and cleanliness.

He kept thinking about his conversation with Aqua Girl, and the more he thought about it, the more unhappy he became. He didn't even like her, not really. But for some reason he kept seeing her face, those too-wide eyes and blond hair and big lips — not fakey lips like from collagen injections, but lips just a fraction bigger than you would expect, like her eyes. And that little scar on her chin.

After a time he succeeded in forcing his thoughts away from her and onto another vexing problem, that of Jerry Preuss. If Wes wasn't careful, Jerry would have him putting up lawn signs, or walking around wearing a sandwich board. Still, Jerry had been his friend since kindergarten, so Wes couldn't just blow him off. He might have to actually do something. Wes stared at the perfectly clean, freshly painted garage floor and focused his mind on the problem. A few minutes later he went to the house, where he found Paula sitting at the kitchen table eating a peanut butter and honey sandwich.

"You're going to spoil your appetite," he said, parroting their mother.

Paula stuck a peanut butter-coated tongue out at him. Wes picked up the phone and dialed Jerry's number.

"I've been thinking about your problem," Wes said when he answered.

"I have a problem?"

"Yeah, you want to get elected president."

"Oh. Yeah."

"Are you ready?"

"I think so."

"T-shirts."

Jerry did not immediately reply.

"T-shirts cost money," he said at last.

"Donations," Wes said. "You ask people for money, then offer to do them special favors if you get voted into office." When Jerry once again did not immediately reply, Wes added, "It's brilliant."

Jerry said, "You know that girl June?"

Wes was confused. "What about her?"

"I was telling her about me running for class president. She had an idea too. She said I should promise people a four-day school week."

"How would you do that?"

"Just promise it, I guess, then worry about how to do it later on. Like real politicians."

"Oh . . . so . . . are you into her?"

"I don't know," said Jerry. "Maybe."

SEVEN

EACH MORNING IT GOT A LITTLE COOLER. At first, June welcomed the early-autumn chill. Walking to school when it was sunny and sixty-two degrees was not so bad. But by the first week of October, the weather had turned colder and rainy, and she had to beg her mom for a ride. Still, she had to walk home after school.

She hadn't talked to floppy-haired Wes since that one day. She saw him in language arts, and sometimes in the hallways between classes, but he always seemed preoccupied, off in his own world.

Phoebe wanted her to hook up with Van Griswold, a vacant but not unattractive jock whose father owned Griswold Motors. Van drove a different car to school almost every week.

"You wouldn't have to worry about walking home from school," Phoebe pointed out. They were sitting in the bleachers after school, watching the track team run drills. Van Griswold was a hurdler, though not a very good one. He ran with short, mincing steps, and his leaps over the hurdles were high and ungainly.

"I tried to talk to him once," June said. "He's kind of dense."

"So? Oh! There's Josh!" Josh Sandstrom, a friend of Van's, also a hurdler, was Phoebe's current love interest. "Go, Josh!" she shouted as he launched himself over the first hurdle. Startled, Josh looked up at precisely the wrong moment; his trailing knee struck the bar, his ankle crumpled, and he collapsed, skidding to a stop on the cinder track.

"Oops," said Phoebe.

"Maybe you shouldn't have yelled," June said.

Phoebe clutched her heart. "Josh . . ."

Josh climbed slowly to his feet. Aside from an ugly scrape on his knee and elbow, he seemed to be okay. As he limped off the track, he looked up at Phoebe and June. His mouth formed a word. They were too far away to hear him, but June was certain the word was "bitch."

Phoebe shrugged. "Oh, crap."

Sometimes, Wes didn't get why he did certain things. Or maybe he did get it, but he just didn't want to think about it. Like changing the way he walked to and from school.

He had given up on the bus unless it was pouring rain. Jerry thought he was nuts, and maybe he was, but the idea of being crammed into a big steel tube with fifty or sixty other kids turned his stomach sour. As for changing his walking route, that had to do with Aqua Girl. In fact, many of Wes's decisions concerning where to go and how to get there were influenced by his wanting to avoid both June and Izzy. He had this feeling about June, like if he got to know her any better his life would get really confusing, especially with Jerry having some sort of thing for her. As for Izzy, he just didn't want to deal with all that history. So he took a roundabout way to school, walking down alleys and cutting through parks and turning his mile-and-a-half walk into two miles.

For a few weeks Wes succeeded in not thinking about it too deeply. Izzy would pop into his head and he would shove her roughly aside, or make himself remember one of her unattractive qualities, like her big saliva-spewing laugh. Thoughts of June were sneakier. He would be thinking about something nice, and suddenly she would be there in his head with those wide-apart eyes, and his guts would stir and his mouth would sort of sag open — all before he realized what was happening. To get rid of June thoughts, he would think about his clean garage, and after a while she would go away and the image in his mind would be that of a perfectly clean, gray painted floor.

It occurred to him on more than one occasion that he might be a little bit crazy. Was he crazy to break up with Izzy? Was he crazy to not ride the bus? Was he crazy to have made the garage as clean and orderly as a hospital surgical unit? Was he any crazier than Jerry, who was planning to become Emperor of the Universe?

Probably. Mr. Varon would think so.

But then, Mr. Varon thought everybody was crazy.

Psych class had sounded really cool when Wes had signed up for it, but Mr. Varon spent most of every period droning on about these old dead guys, as if he was teaching history instead of psychology. Varon would spend thirty minutes going on and on about Sigmund Freud, the supposed father of psychoanalysis, then explain how most of Freud's theories had been flat-out wrong, leaving everybody puzzling over why, if the guy was so full of it, they had to learn about him at all.

Where were the rats and the mazes? Where were the cool experiments on other kids? The hypnosis and stuff? How come he left psych every day in a walking coma instead of, well, *psyched*?

But every so often, Varon came up with something that stuck in Wes's head. Like his theory about all teenagers being nut jobs.

The way Varon explained it, something happened to kids around the age of twelve or thirteen. Their brains got these enormous injections of hormones, and everything got all scrambled and short-circuited, producing what he called "irrational behaviors." Little kids do stupid stuff because they lack information and experience. Teenagers do stupid stuff because their brains are rewiring themselves.

"If, for example," said Mr. Varon, "I were to behave the way many of you do, I would quickly lose my job and be diagnosed as schizophrenic, bipolar, antisocial, and a danger to myself and others. In teens, however, such behavior is tolerated. In other words, insane behavior, in a teen, is considered to be perfectly normal."

Everybody thought that was pretty funny. Aron Brey raised his hand and said, "I hear voices."

"What do they say?" asked Maria Finer.

" 'Kill, kill, kill,' " Aron said.

Mr. Varon did not think that was funny. Actually, neither did anybody else.

"I'm kidding," said Aron.

"Quod erat demonstrandum," said Mr. Varon, which confused the entire class full of bipolar schizophrenics, Wes included.

Still, what Varon said made a weird kind of sense.

June looked at the caller ID on her ringing cell phone. *Ron and Nancy Preuss.* She answered with a cautious "Hello?"

"June? Hi, it's Jerry. Jerry Preuss?"

It took her a second to connect the voice with a face.

"Oh. Jerry?"

"Yeah. How are you doing?"

"Okay," she said. How had he gotten her number?

"I got your number from Naomi Liddell," Jerry said.

"Oh." *Naomi!* "Uh, how's the campaign going?"

"Smooth."

Smooth? "Oh. Good." She could tell he was going to ask her out.

"I wanted to thank you for your suggestion the other day."

Suggestion? "What suggestion?"

"You said I should promise people whatever they want."

"I was sort of kidding."

"Yeah, but it got me thinking. Like, the first thing I have to do is find out what people really want. You know, like do they want a good education, or better cafeteria food, or whatever. So I thought I'd start with you. Seriously. What do you want? I mean, within reason."

I want out of this conversation. "Um, I don't know."

"I was thinking maybe we could get together and talk about it. Because you just seem like a really perceptive person."

June liked that he thought she was perceptive. But was he asking her out, or what?

Jerry said, "For coffee?" When June didn't immediately reply, he added, "It was just an idea."

June imagined Jerry's face with startling clarity, his ears and cheeks reddening, his soft brown eyes tearing up. She heard herself say, "Okay." Because it was such a relief that it was just coffee. She wouldn't have to get dressed up and deal with the whole Big First Date thing — not that she would have said yes to that, but still.

He said, "You know where the Bun and Brew is? We could walk over there tomorrow, from school?"

June thought of Wes, and wondered why she hadn't seen him on the way home lately.

She said, "Okay. Only I have something else I have to do right after school." It wasn't true, but she didn't want to walk to the coffee shop with Jerry. It would feel too public, too exposed. "I could meet you there at three thirty?"

"Deal," said Jerry. "And think about what you want."

"A cappuccino and an éclair," June said.

"I mean as a voter."

June laughed. "Sorry!" She could feel herself relaxing. One thing about Jerry — she would always know what *he* wanted.

EIGHT

ALAN SCHWARTZ PLUNKED HIS TRAY DOWN next to Wes at lunch and said, "Your friend Jerry is a certifiable moron."

"*All* my friends are morons," Wes said.

"Yeah, well, Jerry Preuss makes the rest of us look like Einsteins."

"What did he do?"

"Let's see." Alan sat down, picked up a carrot stick, and counted off his points by tapping it on the table. "Wants to be class president." *Tap.* "An unpaid and thankless position." *Tap.* "Talks about it constantly." *Tap.* "To people who could give a rat's ass." *Tap.* He raised his eyebrows as if to invite disagreement, put the carrot stick in his mouth, and bit down.

"I can't believe you put that thing in your mouth," Wes said.

"I can't believe *Preuss* expects us to listen to his campaign rhetoric for another six months," Alan said through a mouthful of pulverized carrot.

"Wait." Wes sat up straight. "Six *months*?"

"Course. The election is in April. You vote in the class president for the next school year."

Wes shook his head. "The way he's been acting, I thought it was next week."

"Negatory."

"So who's president this year?"

"Laurie Floss."

"Who's Laurie Floss?"

"The budding politician we voted into office last April."

"I don't think I voted anybody into office."

"It was not a highly publicized affair."

"Huh. What did she promise everybody?"

"Nobody knows. But whatever it was, I'm pretty sure we didn't get it."

"So maybe Jerry's strategy of promising everybody everything isn't so stupid after all, if nobody is going to remember it next year."

"What's *stupid* is that he wants to be president in the *first* place. And what were those things he had you handing out?"

Wes shrugged. "Questions for potential voters."

"How come I didn't get one?"

"Did you want one?"

"No!"

"There you go."

"You know what I think?"

"About what?"

"I think all *my* friends are idiots too."

"Oh. My. God. Jerry *Preuss*?" Phoebe made her eyes go huge. "You're totally joking. What was it *like*?"

"We didn't *do* anything," June said, looking from Phoebe to Britt to Jess. "I just went out with him."

"I know. I mean . . . I didn't mean . . . I mean, was he, like . . . or what?"

"He's just a *guy*," June said, wishing she hadn't brought it up at all. "He asked me out — well, first he asked me out for coffee, and then Saturday we went to a movie over at the U. It was sort of cool. Not the movie. But the scene — kind of an older crowd."

"What was the movie?" Britt asked.

"*The Candidate.* A really old Robert Redford movie."

Jess said, "He used to be hot."

"My grandma thinks he's *still* hot," said Britt.

"He wants to be president," June said.

"Robert Redford?"

"No. Jerry. He wants to be class president, and then president of the country." June waited to see what they would say. It was one of those defining moments.

"Oh, well. Van is going out with Kelly Freeman," Phoebe said. Jess and Britt immediately took her remark as permission to accept Jerry Preuss, conditionally.

"Jerry's sort of cute," Jess said. "Except you've got to get him to buy some different glasses."

"Does he have a car?" Britt asked.

"I don't think so," June said. "We took his mom's minivan."

Phoebe said, "Josh and I are going to the outlet mall Saturday."

"I thought he was mad at you," Britt said.

"We made up. I just had to promise not to yell his name at any track meets."

"I bet that's not all you had to promise," Britt said.

"Up yours, bee-yatch," Phoebe said, arching her eyebrows.

"Bitch."

"Bitch."

"Bitch."

They all started laughing. Except for June, at first. But then she started laughing too, even though she didn't exactly get it.

Later, Britt gave June a ride home from school and explained that she, Jess, and Phoebe used to call themselves the Three Bitches. "'One for all and all for one.' Phoebe came up with that back in ninth grade."

"Isn't that from *The Three Musketeers*?" June said.

"You mean the candy bar? What's that got to do with it?"

"Never mind."

"So, Jerry *Preuss*, huh?" Britt said, probing for details.

"He's just a nice guy," June said.

It was true, for once. June's date with Jerry had been right out of *The Concerned Parent's Guide to Correct Teenage Behavior*. Jerry had shown up on time, wearing clean clothes, driving a minivan. He had introduced himself to her parents, told them he was running for class president, that they were going to see *The Candidate* and then for ice cream, and promised to have their daughter home by ten. He had even opened the car door for her.

When June thought back over the evening, she was astounded that she had actually gone through with it. *Minivan?* Movie from the nineteen *seventies?* Ice cream? Home by *ten?* It had promised to be the date from hell, but it wasn't at all. Jerry was dorky, sure, but he knew who he was, and he didn't care what people thought — as long as they would still vote for him for class president. And he was so excited about *that* stupid idea that June had actually gotten into it, brainstorming campaign strategies over mocha malts and talking as if getting Jerry elected was the most important thing in the universe. By the time he kissed her good night at ten minutes before ten — it wasn't the *worst* kiss she'd ever had — she had to admit to herself that it had been a fun night.

"You going to go out with him again?" Britt asked.

"I don't know." She really didn't. If he asked her, she would probably say yes. If he didn't ask her, that would be okay too. "He wants me to be chief strategist for his election campaign."

"Omigod, I saw those flyers or whatever he was handing out. Like, does anybody actually care?"

"Jerry does."

Britt gave her a sideways look. June knew what she was thinking. She was wondering if it was safe to remain friends with somebody who was dating a guy like Jerry Preuss.

Britt pulled up to the curb. For a second, June thought she was going to order her out of the car, but then she realized they had arrived at her house. Funny thing — she'd been living there six weeks and still had to check the house number to be sure it was the right one.

Wes caught up with Jerry at his locker after last period and gave him the rest of the undistributed questionnaires. "I'm not handing out any more of these," Wes said. "You didn't tell me that the election wasn't until April."

Jerry tossed the questionnaires into his locker. "You didn't know that?"

"No!"

"You're my campaign manager. You're supposed to know those things."

"I am *not* your campaign manager."

Jerry did not seem in the least bit bothered. In fact, he seemed unusually confident and imperturbable. "It doesn't matter. I got about twenty of the questionnaires back, and it's pretty clear what people want."

"What's that?"

"Freedom."

"From what?"

"Everything. I'm going to make that my slogan. Freedom!"

"Yeah, well, good luck with that."

"I went out with June Edberg."

Wes suddenly understood what had made Jerry so confident. Going out on a real date was huge for him.

"We went to a movie over at the U," Jerry said. "She's really into politics."

"You going out with her again?"

"Sure. I like her."

"Don't you think her eyes are a little bit too far apart?"

"Are you kidding me? She has fantastic eyes. They're like elf eyes." Before he'd gotten into politics, Jerry had been into *The Lord of the Rings*.

"Elf eyes? Dude. That is so pathetic."

"Yeah, well, I don't see any girls chasing you down the hall."

"Oh, so now she's *chasing* you?"

"I didn't mean that. I just — are you mad at me or something? 'Cause I'm getting this vibe."

"Vibe? Sounds like something my grandpa would say."

Jerry rolled his eyes, as if he was suddenly above it all, as if Wes was some minor annoyance. He closed his locker. "Look, I got a bus to catch. See ya." He walked off. Wes watched him go, astounded that he would walk away like that. He kicked the front of Jerry's locker, leaving a small dent. Jerry and his stupid election and his elf eyes talk and acting so cocky after his big date and everything — it drove Wes crazy. It was . . . well, it was *Jerry*, the way he'd always been: clumsy and nerdy and obsessive and flat-out *irritating*.

Later, walking home, Wes replayed the conversation in his head and couldn't figure out what had made him so mad.

MOST OF THE GUYS JUNE HAD GONE OUT WITH thought it was their sacred duty to attempt to grope every square inch of her body. She was not opposed to a little groping, so long as it did not involve discomfort, bad smells, or excessive bodily fluids. But she didn't enjoy being forced to slap, kick, or yell at her dates.

Jerry was no problem. She'd been with guys who were cuter and sexier and more exciting, but with Jerry she never had to worry about him going all caveman on her. He seemed happy just to be in her presence — and that was both good and bad. He was an intense guy, but most of his intensity was focused on politics. That was good. It meant that if she decided she didn't want to see him anymore, he probably wouldn't fall apart, or become a stalker, or go around telling everybody what a bitch she was. It was important, according to Pragmatic June, to always have an exit strategy.

Until that day came, being with Jerry was okay. They went out once a week, usually to a movie, and they saw each other in school, and sometimes at the coffee shop, and he would call her. Her mom liked Jerry. June's theory was that her mom used her super-mom sense to detect that they weren't having sex or anything. That was all her mom cared about — that her daughter avoid "entanglements."

The Three Bitches, it turned out, were okay with Jerry. Since Phoebe had made up with Josh Sandstrom, they'd gone on a double date. Josh was a nice guy once you got him away from his jock buddies. He and Jerry had discovered a mutual fascination with martial arts movies. Jess and Britt found their own regulars — guys they could count on to hang with them. It was a pretty comfortable arrangement, all in all.

By late October, Jerry had eased off on his election campaign to focus on his schoolwork. June was sailing through her own classes, even physical science. She had thought science would be her worst class, but Mr. Reinhardt was one of those teachers you just couldn't help but listen to, even when he was talking about numbers and stuff that made no sense.

They were studying cosmology — all about the origin of the universe and outer space and gravity and something called dark matter. June didn't understand most of it, but she liked hearing about the Big Bang, how thirteen billion years ago there was nothing. No matter, no space, no time — just a thing called a singularity that was smaller than a grain of salt, yet it contained everything that ever existed. Then the singularity exploded. The explosion was still happening. The Earth and sun and even the galaxy were just tiny fragments, rushing through space at more than a million miles per hour. As strange as all that sounded, June believed it. She didn't *understand* it, but it felt right that she should be riding a spinning chunk of shrapnel headed for nowhere.

By the middle of November, Wes realized that he had fallen behind in school. He began paying attention in his classes, and quickly caught up on his reading. The weather was getting too cold to walk most days, but Alan Hurd got a hand-me-down car

from his mother and started giving him a ride to and from school —
as long as Wes bought him a donut every morning.

Jerry Preuss cooled on his election campaign, at least temporarily. Wes was happy about that, as he had neither the time nor
the inclination to take on any more election-related tasks. As for
Aqua Girl, he saw her in class, and that was it. The sight of her still
stirred up feelings, but it was more like a sense of relief that he
hadn't got mixed up with her.

Izzy he managed to avoid entirely — he heard she was seeing
Thom Samples, a senior.

The garage slowly fell victim to entropy. Small projects undertaken by Wes or his father created nodes of chaos that multiplied
to become larger messes, and then, with the first heavy snows of
mid-November, his mother insisted on parking her car in the
garage, which meant a frantic hour of shoving everything against
the walls or cramming stuff onto shelves, and with the car came
chunks of ice and road salt and mud. The beautiful gray floor
became blackened and gritty. Wes lost interest in the garage and
began spending his spare time hanging out with the two Alans
in Alan Schwartz's basement, playing video games and watching movies and, every now and then, when Calvin Warner and
Robbie Johanson came over, playing poker. Wes lost more than
he won.

One Sunday afternoon in early December, during the first ten
minutes of one of those poker games, Wes lost the entire forty
dollars he had brought. He sat around for a while watching
the others play. Calvin was going on and on about SHC, or
Spontaneous Human Combustion, which is when a person bursts

into flames for no reason. Calvin said it happened all the time; he'd read a book about it.

"They find a pile of ashes where there used to be a person," he said.

"Maybe they were trying to light a fart," said Alan Hurd. "Raise five."

Wes suddenly became disgusted with himself and the whole scene, so he put on his jacket and said, "I gotta go."

Alan Hurd, who had given Wes a ride over, looked up and said, "You gonna *walk*?"

"I guess so," said Wes.

Alan went back to playing his hand. As far as the rest of them were concerned, Wes had already left.

June hated Minnesota. She had hated Illinois, Kansas, Arizona, and Texas, but her most fervent loathing she reserved for Minnesota.

It wasn't the people. People were the same everywhere. Even Jerry Preuss, who had become her unofficial boyfriend, was just another guy with all the niceness, clumsiness, awkwardness, and *irritatingness* of boys everywhere. Jess, Phoebe, and Britt — they were all okay too. And the school was fine — just another school.

But the *weather.* Minnesota was the frozen armpit of the galaxy. *No,* said Scornful June, *it's the frozen* asshole *of the* universe.

Especially on weekends, like this weekend, when she'd planned nothing more than to maybe go to the mall with the Three Bitches, and instead her mom got the Cold from Hell and turned her into Little Miss Home Health Care. Like if June didn't run over to the

SuperAmerica and get her some orange juice in, like, five minutes she would die.

That was the thing with her mom. She tried so hard to be perfect, but let one little thing go wrong — a bad perm, a cold, what*ever* — and she fell apart.

Also, the orange juice in Minnesota tasted like gasoline. Even worse than Kansas and Illinois. She thought about that as she pulled on her parka. Why should the orange juice taste different in Minnesota? Didn't it all come from Florida?

Her hair was a mess, and she didn't have her contacts in so she put on her old eyeglasses, and then she couldn't find her hat. Since she was just running over to the SA and probably wouldn't see anybody, she put on this ridiculous thing of her mom's — a pink knit cap with fuzzy earflaps and an absurdly long tassel — and left for the SA.

It had started snowing again, and it was *cold*, like below-zero cold. Wes turned up his collar, pulled his stocking cap as far down as it would go, jammed his bare hands deep into the pockets of his thin leather jacket, and headed up Garfield Street at a brisk walk. It was even colder and windier than he'd thought, and it was almost four miles to home. The snow was that fine, sharp, crystalline variety that stung like shotgun pellets. Ice crystals found their way down his collar and into his eyes. Soon, he was running with his hands in his pockets, his eyes slitted, his chin buried in his collar, his retro canvas basketball shoes slapping and skidding on the icy sidewalk.

I could die out here, he thought. *I could get frostbite. Hypothermia.*

His right foot hit a patch of glare ice and he fell, landing hard on his hip. For a few seconds he thought he'd broken something, but it was too cold to just lie there, so he got to his feet and started walking. Everything seemed to work, except he was freezing. He looked around. Nothing but anonymous houses — he didn't know anybody in the neighborhood. He kept walking. Three miles to go, at least. Wes had never run three miles in his life, but if he kept walking he would freeze to death for sure, so he broke into a run again. For a few blocks he hardly thought about the cold, but soon he was sweating and wheezing, and he had to stop. The cold slammed into him like a great frozen hammer.

A few blocks ahead were some lights — the SuperAmerica! He could warm up inside the store and call home for a ride. He began to jog again, and a minute later he was inside the SA gasping for breath. As his breathing calmed and his body warmed, he noticed the woman behind the counter staring at him.

"Cold out there," he said with what he hoped was a friendly grin.

The woman shook her head. "You kids don't know how to dress," she said.

"I didn't know I'd be walking," Wes said.

"You kids never think about consequences," she said.

"I know," he said. "Do you have a phone I can use?"

"Pay phone outside," she said.

"I don't have any money."

The woman shook her head. "You kids. Store policy is no free calls."

"Please? I live, like, three miles away from here. I just want to call my mom for a ride."

She made him wait a few more seconds, giving him the evil eye, then sighed as if the responsibility of being an adult was an unbearable weight upon her soul, opened her purse, and handed him her cell phone.

Paula answered on the fourth ring.

"Hey, Paula, it's Wes. Is Mom home?"

"Noper."

"Where is she?"

"She just left for aerobics."

"How long ago?"

"I don't know. Ten minutes?"

That was bad. She wouldn't be reachable for another hour and a half at least. Aerobics class was one of the few times their mom was completely incommunicado.

"Okay, thanks."

"Are you coming home?" Paula asked.

"I'm working on it." He hung up and tried to think who to call next. Maybe Jerry. He started to dial but was interrupted by the counter woman.

"I didn't say you could call the whole phone book. I only have three hundred minutes a month."

Wes handed her the phone.

Ordinarily, June liked driving her mom's BMW, but the trip to the SA with the streets all slippery and snow blowing across the roads was no fun at all, not even in an arctic adventure sort of way. The extreme cold made her think of outer space. Even in deepest space, Mr. Reinhardt said, there was no true vacuum. There might be only one or two atoms per cubic meter of space, but there was always *something*. Atoms were running into each other all the time, like snowflakes. And in a few billion or trillion or centillion years, the Big Bang would reverse direction and atoms would start colliding more often, and eventually they would all be drawn into a single tiny node where every atom in the universe was touching every other atom, and time would stop. According to Mr. Reinhardt, this was called the Big Crunch, when the entire universe became an infinitesimal dot. And then the Big Bang would happen all over again. She found that reassuring — that no matter how messed up the universe got, it would eventually have another chance to get it right.

She was thinking about that as she pulled into the SA and got out and walked through the door.

A girl wearing an enormous down ski parka, fogged-up glasses, and a pink hat with a long tassel entered in a swirl of wind and snow. She walked past Wes, heading for the cooler at the back of the store. She stopped in front of the juice section. It was hard not to look at her, with that hat. The tassel hung all the way down to her thighs, ending in a fuzzy pink ball.

"You kids," said the counter woman. "You think she ever gets that thing caught in a door?"

The girl grabbed a half gallon of orange juice from the cooler. When she turned around, coming back toward the register, Wes recognized her.

"Hey, June," he said.

June pulled up, startled, and dropped the juice. Both she and Wes bent over quickly to get the carton and they banged heads so hard that Wes fell to his knees and, for a second, thought he was going to pass out. He reached up to touch his forehead, expecting to find a bloody mess. There was no blood, but the lump was already forming. June had fallen back on her butt and was sitting with one pink-nailed hand cupped over her left eye.

"Are you okay?" he asked.

"I don't know," she said.

TEN

"LET ME SEE," SAID WES, kneeling in front of her. He gently grasped her wrist and moved her hand away from her eye. He could see right away where his forehead had hit her cheekbone, just below her left eye. It seemed important to get her off the floor, which was dirty and wet from people tracking snow into the store.

"Can you stand up?" he asked.

"I think so."

Wes helped her to her feet.

"My glasses," she said. They found her glasses a few feet away. One lens was cracked and the frames were bent. "They're crunched." June folded them and put them in the pocket of her parka.

"I'm really sorry," Wes said.

"We crunched."

"Uh . . . yeah, we did. I'm sorry."

"Do I need to call nine-one-one?" asked the woman behind the counter.

"I don't . . . I need to look at my face," June said.

The woman pointed toward the back of the store. Wes, still holding her hand, started walking her toward the restrooms, but June shook him off.

"I can walk," she said.

Wes watched her go. He noticed that the end of her pink tassel was filthy — she had fallen on it and ground it into the dirty floor.

"You kids have got to learn to be more careful," the counter woman said.

June thought she had never seen anything so awful as her face in that restroom mirror. It wasn't just the swelling, and the promise of an enormous black eye. It was the whole disgusting package — the pale winter skin, no makeup, dirty hair, and the pink hat. She cleaned up as best she could, then moistened a paper towel and sat on the toilet and pressed the wet towel to her cheek.

She imagined what was waiting for her outside. Wes — floppy-haired Wes — all apologetic and concerned, and that horrible counter woman — she had never liked that woman. But there was no avoiding it. She couldn't stay in the restroom until the end of the universe.

June checked herself in the mirror again. Definitely a black eye coming.

She took her broken glasses from her pocket and tried to put them on her face, but the frame was completely twisted, and the broken lens was worse than nothing. With a sigh, she walked back out into the store. Wes was still standing by the front counter.

"Your OJ," he said, holding up the carton of juice.

Wes wasn't sure what to expect. Would she be mad at him? Would she be crying? Would she have to go to the emergency room?

June took the orange juice from him, put it on the counter, dug in her jeans pocket, and came out with a five-dollar bill. The counter woman rang up the sale and gave her change. Wes stood by helplessly.

"I'm really sorry," he said.

June turned to him and held up her broken glasses.

"I can't see. You have to drive me home." She didn't seem angry.

"I don't have a car," he said.

"In *my* car." Not angry, but she wasn't smiling.

If anything, it was even colder and windier outside. They got into the car.

"I've never driven a BMW before," Wes said.

"It's just a car."

Wes turned the key in the ignition.

"I don't know where you live."

"On Twentieth."

"Oh." That was where he thought she lived. He backed out of the parking space, then stopped. She was shaking. "Are you okay?" He realized she was laughing.

"I can't believe that happened!" she said between gasps.

Then Wes cracked up too, and a second later he realized he'd let his foot off the brake and they were about to roll into one of the gas pumps. He hit the brake just in time, and June started laughing even harder.

"You . . . almost . . . wrecked . . . the car!" she said, her eyes tearing up.

Wes, caught between embarrassment and laughter, put the car in drive and pulled out onto the street.

"That would have been perfect," June said, then hiccupped.

Wes thought that was the funniest thing he'd ever heard and had to pull over. He bumped the curb.

June looked at him in mock shock, one eye wide, the other one beginning to swell shut. Her eyes were a pale, icy blue, not the aqua he remembered. "You are the worst driver *ever*," she said, and for no reason at all, that set them both off again.

It was only about a mile to June's house. On the way, June told him about her mom's Cold from Hell and of her urgent demand for orange juice.

"I just hope my mom appreciates I got a concussion for her orange juice," June said.

"Everybody appreciates a good concussion." Wes put a hand to the lump on his forehead.

"It's the house with the ginormous Santa."

Wes pulled into the driveway. There was a sparkly wreath on the door and a six-foot plastic Santa Claus guarding the front steps.

"Nice Santa," Wes said.

"I know. It's embarrassing." She leaned across him and activated the garage door opener clipped to the visor. "Can you pull into the garage?"

They drove into the garage and got out.

"Thanks for driving me home," June said. She looked him over and frowned. "Is that all you're wearing?"

"I live pretty close to here."

"Yeah, like a *mile*."

"You know where I live?"

"You told me you lived on Fourteenth. When we were walking home."

"I did?" That she actually remembered made him feel warm inside.

"Give me a minute to OJ my mom and put in my contacts and I'll drive you home. You want to come in? I have to warn you, my mom has been filling the entire house with cold virus."

"I'll risk it," said Wes.

CHAPTER ELEVEN

NATURALLY, HER MOM FREAKED.

"Oh my God, what happened?" She sat up in bed. "Are you okay?"

"Obviously not," June said, setting the glass of orange juice on the bedside table. "I have a black eye."

"I mean — oh my God, did you have a car accident?"

"Your car is fine," said June. She told her mom what had happened.

"Junie, you have to be more careful."

"Thanks. I'll remember that."

"Let me see."

June leaned closer and let her mom examine her injury.

"You have to get some ice on it."

"I know. I had to bring you your orange juice first."

"Oh, Junie!" Her mom picked up the glass of orange juice and sipped. "There's a bag of frozen peas in the freezer. Use that."

Wes was sitting on one of the stools when June got back to the kitchen. She opened the freezer and found the peas. She held the bag to her cheek and sat down next to Wes.

"I don't think I can drive with one eye," she said.

Wes leaned closer and looked straight into her face. She moved the ice pack aside to show him.

"They're different colors," he said.

"What?"

"Your eyes. Your right eye is aqua colored, and the other one is more like light blue."

"Which do you like better?"

"I like both."

"The right one is my contact. It's tinted. The other contact I can't get in."

"How did you get that little scar?"

"Snakebite."

"Really?"

"Stray bullet. Knife fight. Grizzly attack. Stray meteorite."

Wes imagined each event.

"Exploding clown shoes."

That was when he kissed her.

Later, Wes would wonder what had made him do it. But at the time, it was as if an enormous soft hand had pressed him toward her, and their lips had touched, and he heard his heart beating, once, twice, three times. He heard the bag of peas fall to the floor, and then it was over and they were staring at each other from about four inches apart. Her pupils were so big they nearly filled her irises, and the smell of her was making him dizzy.

"Oh no," said Wes.

They pulled farther apart.

June said, "I didn't . . ."

Wes stood up clumsily, knocking the stool over. He picked it up and set it back in place, then he picked up the bag of frozen peas and handed it to her.

"It's okay," said June.

"Look, I didn't mean to —"

"It's *okay*," June said. "Just . . ." She fluttered her hand, as if waving him off. Wes turned to go, but she said, "Don't go."

Wes didn't know what to do, so he stood there, halfway to the door, looking back at her. She returned the bag of peas to her face.

Wes stared. The dirty, mussed-up hair, the swollen, discolored cheek, the two different-colored eyes — none of it mattered.

"You look nice," he said, and he meant it.

June's mouth stretched and her eyes squeezed shut and she was laughing and her eyes were watering. Wes stood helplessly by as she brought herself under control.

He said, "I don't think I ever knew anybody who could do that. Laugh and cry all at once."

"It hurts to laugh." June wiped her good eye with the back of her hand. "Please don't be funny."

"I wasn't trying to be."

"That's what made it funny."

"I think I should go."

"I know. Only I'm afraid you'll freeze to death."

They heard the side door open. A man's voice called out, "Who left the garage door open?"

"My dad," said June.

A few seconds later June's father, a tall, handsome man with graying temples and an unseasonal tan, stepped into the kitchen.

Mr. Edberg looked from Wes to June, then back at Wes, then smiled, showing a vast number of brilliant white teeth, and said in a booming voice, "Well, hello, Jerry! Good to see you again, son."

"Daddy, this is *Wes*."

"Wes!" He gave Wes another look over. "You look like that young man Jerry."

"No, he doesn't, Daddy. He's nothing like Jerry at all."

Wes held out his hand. "I'm Wes Andrews, sir."

"Wes! Wes! Of course! Elton Edberg." They shook hands.

Mr. Edberg looked at June and frowned. "Junie, why are you holding peas on your face?"

June took the bag away from her eye and showed him.

CHAPTER
TWELVE

WES SAT QUIETLY IN THE PASSENGER SEAT as they backed out of the garage. He had the feeling he was about to have an awkward conversation. Mr. Edberg did not disappoint him.

"So, Wes," he said, "you gave my daughter a black eye."

"It was an accident," Wes said.

"There are no accidents, son. Only the unforeseen consequences of reckless behavior."

"Yes, sir."

"You're very polite. I like that."

"Thank you."

Mr. Edberg laughed. "I'm just messing with you, Wes."

"Yes, sir."

"Call me Elton. Or El."

"Okay."

"Tell me again where you live?"

"On Fourteenth." Wes gave him the address.

"What do your folks do?"

"My dad's a manager at Anderson Distributing. My mom's a part-time teacher over at St. Mary's."

"Your mother is a nun?"

"No. She —"

"Just messing with you, son." Mr. Edberg laughed again.

Wes did not like the man.

"Yes, sir," he said.

"Please, call me El."

"Okay." There was no way.

"So, Wes, are you the new Jerry?"

Wes didn't know what to say, so he said nothing.

"Or has my little girl got a stable of young studs in waiting?"

Wes said, "Mr. Edberg, sir, June and I bonked heads at the SA, and she couldn't see, so I drove her home. That's all."

Mr. Edberg shook his head. "Wes, I make my living by reading people's hopes and desires . . . turn here?"

"Yeah."

". . . and their fears. I know things about you that even you don't know. You might think that you're telling me the truth, but you would be wrong. Which house?"

"The one with the big oak tree in front."

Mr. Edberg pulled into the driveway.

As Wes got out, Mr. Edberg smiled broadly and said, with utter sincerity, "Sorry I gave you a hard time, Wes. It's my job."

"Yes, sir," said Wes.

Paula wanted to know why he had a bump on his head.

"Because I bumped it," he said.

"Are you having a concussion?"

"No, I'm fine."

"Then how come you're acting weird?"

"I'm not."

"Are too."

Wes tipped his head back and squeezed another rope of honey into his mouth.

"That's gross," Paula said.

"Tough."

"Did you know honey is the same as bee spit?"

Wes twisted the cap back onto the squeeze bottle and put the honey back in the cupboard.

"I'm gonna tell Mom you ate all the bee spit."

"No, you're not."

"How do you know?"

"I'm older. I know things about you that even you don't know."

"Do not."

"Is Mom still at aerobics?"

"Yupper."

"I'm going to my room."

"That's all you ever do. Mom says you're like the Phantom of the Opera."

"Whatever." Wes bounded up the stairs to his bedroom and closed the door and sat on his bed. A few seconds later he heard the blare of the television. He and Paula used to watch a lot of TV together, Paula asking a thousand questions, Wes making up goofy answers. Sometimes, Izzy had been there, and Paula had asked her the questions. Izzy's answers had always been better than his.

He imagined watching TV with June and Paula. Would Paula like June? Would June be patient and funny like Izzy? Would she call Paula "Paulalicious"? No, that would be too creepy. He moved Paula out of the picture and settled into an imaginary sofa in front of an imaginary TV with June by his side. He put an imaginary arm around her and looked into her one good eye and — *no!* He couldn't go there, not even in his head. She was Jerry's girlfriend — Jerry's first girlfriend ever. It would kill him to lose her. Especially to Wes. And even though Wes knew that Jerry and June could not possibly last much longer, he did not want to be the one to end it. The only way he could imagine himself with June was after a disaster. Say she broke up with Jerry and moved away, and then one day Wes was, um, flying to Hawaii, and June happened to be on the same flight, and the plane crashed, and the two of them made it to an island on one of the life rafts and built a hut on the beach. . . .

Paula was right; he *was* being weird.

June was staring at her reflection in her bedroom mirror when Jerry called.

"Hey," he said.

"Hey, yourself."

"What did you do today?"

"Nothing. I, um . . ." She didn't want to tell him about her black eye. Even though he'd see it sooner or later. How long does a black eye take to clear up? A couple days? And why do they call it a black eye? It's not really black. More like purple and violet and blue and red. Later, there would be yellow and green. Maybe she could cover it up with makeup. "This weather really sucks," she said.

"I know. You have much homework this weekend?"

"Yeah, some." *This is the most boring conversation I think I've ever had.* "I'm supposed to write that thing for English?"

"I have to do that too."

"And a take-home quiz for science. I already did it. It was easy."

"You want to do something tonight?"

No! "I'm kind of tired."

"I could probably get my dad's SUV. Maybe I could come over and hang out?"

No, no, no! "Um . . . remember I told you my mom has this cold? Actually, I think I might have it too." She sniffed and cleared her throat.

"Oh. Okay. You want me to bring over some hot herbal tea? My mom swears by herbal tea."

"I've got tea. I'd just as soon sit here with my Kleenexes and teddy bear."

"You have a stuffed bear?"

"Yeah. Actually it's just a little thing on my key chain." *Please, God, get me out of this conversation.* "His name is Bernard."

"Oh. Okay."

"Anyways, I don't really feel like company."

"Oh. Okay."

After she hung up, June noticed that she was getting a little snuffly for real. The thought that she might be getting her mom's cold cheered her — if she could skip the next couple of school days, her eye might clear up, and she wouldn't have to deal with all the explanations. She wouldn't have to see Jerry. Or Wes. She could just pretend that nothing had ever happened because, really, nothing actually had.

THIRTEEN

WES HAD BEEN EXCITED AND SCARED about seeing June in school on Monday, so he was both disappointed and a little relieved when she didn't show up. He was trying to figure out a way to find out why — was she in the hospital? — when Jerry came up to him as he was loading some books into his locker and told him June had stayed home with a cold.

"Huh," said Wes, as if there was no earthly reason he should care about the state of June Edberg's health.

"I suppose that means I'll get it too," said Jerry.

"That's the problem with having a girlfriend."

"Yeah." Jerry nodded. "I suppose you pretty much get the same diseases. Was it like that when you were with Izzy?"

"We were both sick all the time," Wes said.

"I'll probably go see her after school. See how she's doing."

"I wouldn't, at least not until the nose-dripping stage is over."

"I don't mind getting *her* cold," Jerry said.

"Yuck." Wes was genuinely repulsed.

"I know," Jerry said. "I think that's how you know you're in love. When you even like the yucky stuff."

Even before he knew he was going to do it, Wes smacked Jerry on the top of his head.

"Ow!" Jerry ducked away. "What was that for?"

"Dope slap," Wes said. "For being a dope."

Jerry rubbed his head. "That was kind of hard for a dope slap."

"You were being extra dopey."

"Oh yeah?" Jerry swung, trying to deliver his own dope slap, but Wes caught his arm and twisted it. Jerry yelled and swung at Wes with his free hand, but Wes blocked it and shoved him up against the wall of lockers. The back of Jerry's head hit the edge of Wes's locker door with a loud *tok*. He slid down onto his butt, eyes unfocused, leaving a streak of bright red blood on the front of the locker.

Wes backed away, becoming aware of a gathering crowd. A pair of hands grabbed Wes from behind and pulled him roughly back. Ms. Mayer, one of the librarians, crouched down beside Jerry. "Jerry? Can you hear me?"

Jerry did a bobblehead imitation, head lolling.

"Jerry?"

His hands flopped like a pair of beached carp.

Ms. Mayer had her cell phone out and was dialing 911.

The man holding Wes was Mr. Johnson, the music teacher. He pulled Wes down the hallway toward the office.

"What was that about?"

"Nothing." Wes couldn't believe what had happened. "We were just goofing around."

A few years ago — he'd been nine — Wes had fallen out of the oak tree in his front yard and broken his leg so badly that the bone stuck out through his skin. Nothing before or since had ever hurt so bad, or been so frightening. He remembered every detail — screaming in pain, his mom rushing outside and finding him, the ambulance ride, and the surgery. His parents told him he'd been unconscious for that part, but he was sure he remembered it — the horrible pulling and grinding sensation when they set his shinbone back into place. It had been the worst day of his life.

Until now.

Wes leaned forward in the flimsy plastic chair and hung his head over his knees. He heard a distant siren. All of them — Mr. Johnson, the secretaries, everybody who came in the door — looked at him like he was this monster. The violent, ugly beast who had attacked Jerry Preuss. He would rather be lying on the ground with a bone sticking out through his shin than have them look at him that way.

The siren got louder, and then it stopped. He imagined the ambulance at the front entrance, EMTs pushing through the glass doors of the foyer with a gurney. The thought of Jerry's face when he slid down that wall made Wes want to throw up. What if he was seriously hurt? And what the hell had *happened*? One second they were just talking and all of a sudden Jerry was *swinging* at him. Sure, Wes had given him a little dope slap, but they did that stuff all the time, just kidding around, no big deal . . . it was *never* a big deal.

And what was it with everybody all of a sudden getting hit on the head? First he and June bonked each other, and now Jerry . . . how was it always his fault? He stared down at the floor. It was filthy. Hundreds of students tromping in with dirty snow on their feet. It could have happened to any one of them. Just goofing around and somebody gets hurt. He thought of the woman at the SuperAmerica. *You kids* . . .

It was just as much Jerry's fault. For that matter, it was partly June's fault because if Jerry hadn't been acting so moony eyed over her he wouldn't have needed a dope slap. And what would *she* think when she heard that he had put her boyfriend — his oldest friend — in the hospital? He had to call her and explain what happened, that he hadn't meant for Jerry to get hurt, and that it wasn't his fault.

June really did have her mom's cold, which was freaky because she had been all psyched to fake it so she could stay home from school. Did she get the cold because she had wanted it? Her dad would think so. Her dad was all into the power of positive thinking. He told his clients that the first step to success was to imagine it.

"If you can imagine it, you're halfway there," he liked to say.

Maybe he was right. She'd gotten sick because she had imagined it.

Whatever the case, her nose was running like a faucet and her throat was sore. She spent most of the day in bed drinking herbal tea and flipping through back issues of *Cosmo* and *People*. She didn't even turn her cell on. Around three o'clock, Jerry called the house phone. Her mom answered it and brought the phone to her room.

"Tell him I'm sleeping," June said.

She must have looked really pathetic because her mom just nodded, took her hand off the mouthpiece, cleared her throat, and said, "I'm sorry, Jerry. June is taking a nap."

Thank you, June mouthed.

A little later the phone rang again.

"If it's for me, I'm sleeping!" It hurt her throat to yell.

Sometime later — it was getting dark out — June shuffled to the bathroom, still in her pajamas and slippers, for another dose of cold medicine. Her mom heard her and called out, "I made chicken noodle soup, Junie."

Chicken noodle soup. The thought of those fat noodles sliding down her throat almost made her gag. She swallowed the cold medicine and walked to the kitchen for a glass of orange juice. Her mother, wearing her auburn wig, full makeup, and a dark green jacket and dress ensemble — what she called her "money outfit" — was sorting through her purse.

"You're going somewhere?" June asked, surprised.

"I'm helping your father with a management seminar tonight, then we're having dinner with some of the Sani-Made executives. Have you seen my car keys?"

June thought for a moment, then looked at the hooks door, where the keys were supposed to be hung. "Isn't that them?"

Her mother looked at the keys and made an exasperated sound with her lips.

"I swear I'm losing it," she said. "Who'd have thought that I would actually hang my keys up?"

"You didn't. I told Wes to put them there."

"Wes? Oh yes. The boy who blackened your eye. He called, by the way. I told him you were doing a Camille." "Doing a Camille" was what her mom called it when June pretended to be extra miserable. Something about an old movie, older even than her mother.

"You didn't really."

"No, I told him you were sleeping."

"Oh."

"I wrote his number down." She pointed at the notepad by the kitchen phone. "He said to tell you, 'It wasn't my fault.'"

"What wasn't his fault?"

"I have no idea."

After her mother left, June ladled some soup into a bowl, picked out the noodles, and ate what was left. It was okay. Not that she could taste anything.

It wasn't my fault.

What had Wes meant by that? That he'd bumped heads with her and given her a black eye? That he'd kissed her? What did he mean?

She considered calling him. Ask him what he meant. Would that be like chasing him? What about Jerry?

She wished she knew how long she would be living here. Her dad only had a six-month contract with Sani-Made, and sometimes these jobs ended early. They might be gone in a month or two, and then it wouldn't matter what she did because she would be gone and all the names and numbers on her cell phone would be erased and she would have to start over. But if they stayed longer — her dad *always* promised that they would settle down — then she would have to decide what to do and live with it.

Jerry was easy.

Jerry was comfortable.

Jerry was a nice guy.

Jerry was Wes's friend.

Wes had kissed her.

A good kiss. The kind of kiss that said, *I want you. I need you.* As if it took every last ounce of his willpower to keep from tearing her clothes off and doing it right there on the kitchen floor.

Jerry had never kissed her like that. And if he had, she wouldn't have liked it.

But she had liked that kiss from Wes.

It wasn't my fault, he had said.

June tore the top sheet off the notepad, went to her room, and entered Wes's number into her cell phone. So she would have it. Just in case she ever needed it. She noticed that there were several missed calls. Three from Jerry, one from Phoebe, and one from Britt. She turned her cell off and got into bed and closed her eyes and tried to make it all go away. All of it.

All but that kiss.

FOURTEEN

JERRY WAS OKAY. He had a "possible mild concussion" and a cut on the back of his head. They stitched him up and sent him home after just three hours at the hospital.

"Thanks for calling, I guess," Jerry said.

"I'm really sorry," Wes said.

"You should be," said Jerry. "I still have a headache."

"Well, *I* got suspended. My parents are really pissed. I'm stuck in the house for the rest of the week."

"Too bad." Jerry wasn't going to let him off easy.

"I don't know what happened," Wes said. "We were just goofing around, and —"

"And you smacked me."

"It was supposed to be like a dope slap. I don't even remember why I did it. I didn't mean for it to be so hard."

"Well, it was."

"Then when you tried to hit me back, I guess I got mad."

Jerry didn't say anything.

"Jer? You there?"

"Ever since you broke up with Izzy, you've been acting like a jerk," Jerry said. "Maybe you should make up with her."

"She's going out with Thom Samples. Besides, I don't want to. Izzy was cramping my style."

Jerry laughed. "Your *style*? Since when do you have a style to be cramped?"

Wes was nettled. If he could have reached his arm through the phone, he would have delivered another dope slap.

"You know what I mean," he said.

"Actually, I don't. Even June has noticed it."

"June didn't even *know* me when I was with Izzy."

"Yeah, but she noticed how weird you've been acting."

"What did she say?"

"I don't know. We were talking about you, and —"

"When?"

"I don't know. A few days ago. Anyway, she said you walk around like you don't care what anybody thinks. Like you think you're better than everybody else."

"She said that?"

"Something like that."

Wes could feel his entire body tensing up. Was that really what June thought?

"Have you talked to her today?" he asked.

"She's still home sick. I tried her a few times, but she must still be sleeping."

"What are you going to tell her? I mean, about what happened today."

"Just the truth — that you slammed me against the wall so hard I woke up in the hospital. Why? What does it matter to you? I mean, since you don't care what anybody thinks."

"I just don't want people to get the wrong idea."

"Then you shouldn't be pushing people around."

"What? I didn't . . . look, it wasn't my fault. You were trying to hit me."

"Yeah, right. You know, Wes, you should get therapy or something."

June got out of bed and went to the kitchen and stared at the telephone until it stopped ringing. She knew it was Wes, from the caller ID. She waited a minute, then picked up the phone and checked the voice mail. No messages.

It wasn't my fault.

She could have picked up the phone and found out what he meant. Or she could call him back, right now, and in a few minutes she would know.

She practiced saying, "Hi, Wes? It's me." Would he know who "me" was? "My mom said you called?" Her voice sounded wrong. She sounded like she was holding her nose. He would laugh — she could hear it already. Well, what did he expect? She had a cold. People with colds talk funny.

The phone rang again. It was Jerry. She let it ring. What had people done before caller ID? It must have been awful to pick up a phone never knowing who was on the other end. The ringing stopped. Next he would call her cell phone. Again. Jerry was like that. Persistent.

It was nearly midnight when her parents got home. June could hear snatches of their conversation as they got ready for bed. It sounded as if their dinner with the Sani-Made executives had not gone well.

"They're all scared to death you're going to get them fired," her mom said.

"Sani-Made has a very top-heavy payroll," said her dad.

"You didn't need to bring that up at dinner. You made everyone very uncomfortable."

June had noticed that when things were not going well, her mother always said "you." *You shouldn't have blah-blah-blah*, or *You get what you pay for*. But when things went well, it was always "we" and "our." *We really did a great job. Our presentation was spot on.*

June had learned about that in psychology. It was called *attribution*. When something good happens, people like to take credit for it. *I got a raise because I did a good job*. But when things go bad, that same person likes to *attribute* it to outside forces. *I got fired because my boss is a jerk.*

Her mom was a major league attributor.

June was not much of an attributor herself. She believed that things just happened, and all you could do was deal with it. Like hitting heads with Wes Andrews, or catching a cold, or moving to a new city.

Her eye would clear up whether she did anything or not.

Her cold would go away.

She would go back to school.

Her parents would pack up and move again.

The universe would contract.

FIFTEEN

THE NEXT DAY IT DIDN'T SEEM SO URGENT that he talk to June. Jerry had probably already told his side of the story — or she had heard it from Phoebe or one of those other girls she hung out with. She would believe it, or she wouldn't. If she wanted to know what had really happened, she would call him back. And if she didn't want to know, then he didn't care what she thought.

Wes spent most of the day reading a book of "great American short stories" for English. He started out with the shortest story in the book, then read the next shortest, and so on. Some of them were pretty good, but a lot of them he didn't get what the big deal was, especially the ones where in the end the character figures out that life just plain sucks, which Wes could have told them going in. After a while he got sick of reading and started thinking about calling June again. Maybe she was sitting around nursing her cold, bored out of her mind, wishing the phone would ring. Twice he picked up the phone but didn't get as far as actually punching in her number.

That night, after a long and uncomfortable dinner with his parents, Wes shut himself in his room, got on his computer, and did a search for June Edberg. There were a few June Edbergs, but never the right one. He did find her father's website: *Elton Edberg*

Consultants — Workout and Bankruptcy Specialists. No mention of June on the website, but there were lots of pictures of her dad, always with that same big, white, sharky smile.

Every hour, like clockwork, June went from her bed to the bathroom to the kitchen — the Bermuda Triangle of staying home sick, from bored to boringer to boringest. Her face looked awful — the bruised area had taken on a greenish cast, and there was a speck of red at the corner of her eye, a ruptured blood vessel. Her entire face hurt when she coughed. She was coughing a lot.

Her mother had declared herself completely recovered and was off doing something businessy. Right about the time he would be getting out of school, Jerry called. She was finally bored enough to welcome his call.

"Hey," she said, sitting up in bed.

"How are you feeling?" he asked.

"Terminal. What's going on?"

"Nothing. Except I got in a fight with Wes."

"You did?" June wasn't sure she'd heard him right. "You mean like an argument?"

"No, like he slammed my head against a locker. I had to go to the hospital and get X-rays and stitches."

"Seriously? Are you okay?"

"Yeah."

"I thought you guys were friends. Why would he do that?"

"I don't know. I think he's having some kind of mental problems."

"Wow."

"He got kicked out for the rest of the week. Are you coming to school tomorrow?"

Tomorrow was too soon. She was hoping she could milk her cold for a few more days to give her eye time to heal. "I don't think so. You really don't know why he did that?"

"No. We were just talking — talking about you, actually — and all of a sudden he was calling me names and then he hit me and the next thing I knew, I woke up in the ambulance."

"You were talking about me?"

"I think so."

"Oh." *It wasn't my fault.* "By the way, just so you know, I have sort of a black eye. I —" June looked around her bedroom. "I got out of bed in the middle of the night and tripped and my face hit the doorknob. So I look like somebody beat me up too."

Thursday night, June's mother insisted that June return to school the next day.

"I haven't heard you cough in hours," she said.

June knew from the tone in her mother's voice that it was nonnegotiable, but she tried faking a cough anyway. Her mom laughed.

The next morning, June got up extra early and went to work on her face. After half an hour of experimenting, she got it to the point where no one would be able to tell she had a black eye. Instead, they would think she was going to a Halloween party. She had slathered on so much foundation that her face felt as if it might slide right off her skull. To keep it from cracking, she would have to avoid smiling, frowning, talking, or eating. Was that even possible?

Her mother was sitting in the breakfast nook with a cup of coffee. She watched wordlessly as June poured a cup of coffee for herself and stirred in four teaspoons of sugar and a glug of cream. June faked a cough, then put a slice of bread in the toaster and stood watching it as she sipped her pale coffee.

Her mother said, "You might do better to just let them see your eye."

June did not reply. She wanted her mom to feel bad about sending her to school, even if it meant she had to look like a clown all day.

"I can give you a ride if you want."

"No, thanks," said June.

The toast popped up. June carefully buttered it, making sure that every square millimeter was covered.

"Or, if you want, you can just take my car."

June looked at her mom. "Really?"

"I won't need it today."

"Thanks," said June. She smiled and felt the foundation at the corners of her mouth crack.

June was halfway to school when it occurred to her that she could just skip. The office had called on Monday, and her mother had told them June would be out for "a few days." They wouldn't call again. She could do whatever she wanted — spend the day at the mall, see a movie, sit in a Starbucks and guzzle cappuccinos, hang out at the library — anything would be better than going to school with a clown face.

As for Jerry, that old saying — "Absence makes the heart grow fonder" — was completely untrue. She hadn't seen him since last Friday, and with each passing day, she wanted to see him less. It was hard enough talking on the phone, listening to him go on and on about his political career, but now he was on this anti-Wes kick, talking about everything Wes had ever done going back to kindergarten. The more he told her things — like how Wes had once broke Jerry's G.I. Joe, and how he'd once put chewing gum in Jerry's hair, and how he'd talked Jerry into stealing a Batman comic and abandoned him when he got caught — the wimpier and whinier Jerry seemed.

It began to make sense to her that Wes had slammed him up against the wall.

She turned on Fourteenth Street and drove past Wes's house. A giant oak tree was growing in the middle of the front yard. She drove around the block and passed the house again. Wes was in that house, probably still asleep. She wondered which window was his bedroom.

She would have driven by a third time, but that would have felt too much like stalking, so instead she drove over to the Starbucks on Front Street, by the college, where she was pretty sure she wouldn't see anyone she knew.

After days of not leaving the house once, Wes was ready to start chewing his way through the walls. So when his mom left to go to a meeting at St. Mary's, saying she wouldn't be back until five or so, he put on his jacket and hat and went for a walk. It was cold out, but not nearly as bad as the last time he'd tried to walk someplace — the day he'd bumped heads with June.

He walked fast, staring at the sidewalk, avoiding the icy patches, avoiding the cracks, enjoying the jolt that every step sent up his spine to the base of his skull. He would not think about Jerry. He would not think about June. He would not think about Izzy and Thom Samples. Instead, he thought about what it would be like when he moved out. When he went to college. Or — forget college — when he got a job and an apartment with a balcony, where he could sit and watch the people passing on the street below. He would keep his apartment very clean and orderly. He would get a very cool job. Something high-tech, where he could make lots of money. Or maybe the opposite — go to Tahiti and work on a fishing boat and live in a shack on the beach. The exact opposite of Minnesota. As his heels hammered the frozen sidewalk, he tried to imagine the feel of warm sand and ocean breezes.

He liked walking. Maybe he would walk across the country, find someone to sponsor him. Walk to cure cancer or something. Start right after school. No, forget that. Forget school. He could start out in March and head straight south. March wouldn't be so bad. Better yet, he could fly to Seattle and start walking southeast. Walk all the way to Key West, the very tip of Florida. He could walk it in a few months.

The sidewalk widened. Wes looked up. He had moved from his own middle-class neighborhood of modest bungalows into a neighborhood of larger, newer homes. He kept moving, trying to figure out what street he was on. Had he turned left or right off Thirteenth Street? He stopped and looked around. His eyes caught on a familiar house with a wreath on the door and a huge plastic Santa standing guard.

His stomach swirled. He turned quickly and started back the way he'd come.

Too late. He recognized the car coming up the street, slowing to turn into the driveway.

He raised his head and waited for her to recognize him.

CHAPTER SIXTEEN

June pulled over to the curb and stared through the passenger window at Wes. Right in front of her house. He looked back at her with this odd expression, like his brain had locked up and needed to reboot. After a few seconds, he climbed over the pile of snow at the curb and opened the door and got in. June put the car back in gear and pulled away. Neither of them spoke until they were a few blocks away.

"I didn't know where I was," Wes said. "Until I saw the giant Santa."

June did not say anything. Her brain was going too fast for words.

"Where are we going?" he asked.

June said, "Coffee." Because it was all she could think of.

"Not at the B and B."

"No, someplace else." She drove straight, stopping at the stop signs, then driving straight some more until she didn't know where they were. She pulled over and stopped.

"I'm lost," she said, looking out through the windshield.

"We're a few blocks from the freeway."

"I don't really want coffee," she said.

"Me neither."

June lowered her eyes to the dashboard. The lights and

dials meant nothing. She turned off the car. She thought he was staring at her, at her cracking makeup, but she did not look at him.

He said, "Your eye looks better."

"It's the makeup."

"Did you go to school today?"

"I skipped."

"Me too. Well, actually I'm suspended."

June said nothing.

"I go back Monday," Wes said.

"Me too."

"I called you."

"I know. I'm sorry I didn't call you back."

"I got in a fight with Jerry."

"Jerry told me."

"It was an accident."

June said nothing.

He said, "We were just messing around. I don't know what happened."

"It's okay," said June.

"Look at me."

She turned her face toward him.

"You got both your contacts in," he said.

June nodded. She was having trouble breathing. His hand reached out and touched her cheek, a touch as soft as a breeze. She became acutely aware of her body, of every square centimeter of her skin, of the sound of air molecules striking her eardrums.

"Does it still hurt?"

"No."

Wes lowered his hand to his lap, but he did not take his eyes off her.

After a few heartbeats, she said, "What are we going to do?"

What was it about this girl, this fish girl with her fake aqua eyes too far apart and that thick layer of makeup? Wes could feel the pressure building in his throat, in his chest, in his groin, as if he was about to explode. Spontaneous Human Combustion. He had never felt this way around Izzy. His fingers still tingled where he had touched her cheek.

"I don't know," he said. His voice sounded thick. He reached for her again, but stopped just before he touched her. His hand was shaking.

Her eyes moved from his face to his hand. She grasped his fingers and pressed the back of his hand to her cheek.

"Your hand is cold," she said.

Wes drew a shaky breath and closed his eyes. He took back his hand and let his head fall back against the headrest and kept his eyes closed. It helped that he couldn't see her. He let out his breath and breathed in again. Maple syrup and fresh-turned soil. He felt things crumbling inside.

June's eyes explored his face — his floppy hair sticking out from underneath the stocking cap, the sparse whiskers on his chin and along his jaw, his long eyelashes, the way his lips curved up at the corners even when he wasn't smiling. Why was he sitting with his eyes closed?

The windows were fogged up. When had that happened? No

one could see in or out, and Wes had his eyes shut. She was the only one who could see.

"What are you thinking?" she asked quietly.

He didn't reply at first. She wondered if he had heard her. Then his tongue peeked out and moistened his lips and he said, "I can't breathe when I look at you."

"Thanks a lot!"

"I'm serious. You're just too . . . too, I don't know."

June was having trouble breathing too. Maybe it was carbon monoxide. She rolled her window down and inhaled a lungful of ice-cold outside air. When she turned back to Wes, he had opened his eyes. He was staring at her again. He looked frightened.

"I gotta" — his voice cracked — "go." Then he was out the door and running away.

SEVENTEEN

WES WAS PROFOUNDLY EMBARRASSED. By the time he reached Astin Boulevard, he was gasping for breath and the red in his face was from exertion. He slowed down to a fast walk. His heels hitting the sidewalk shifted something inside him; his embarrassment became more akin to anger. Why had she come driving up the street, surprising him like that? Why had he gotten into the car with her? Just when he was getting things straight in his head, when he was ready to go back to school and just do the work and avoid getting all snarled up, Aqua Girl, Fish Girl . . . no, *Spider* Girl shows up to get him all tangled in her web. And then she made him act like a crazy person, running off like a scared little kid. And now he was going to get home late and his mom would probably be there, and there'd be a whole scene about him supposedly being grounded and irresponsible and God knows what all else. And Jerry, it was his fault too. And the whole school thing, having to go back on Monday and face everybody. He wished he could strap a bomb to his chest. An atomic bomb, to vaporize his every last molecule. That would take care of it.

The thought of being vaporized calmed him. His breathing eased, and he could feel his heart slowing. Fish Girl. Maple syrup girl. Girl with the black eye — and blue eyes, two different blues. He didn't even *know* her, not really. For all he knew, she might be a drug addict, a toenail biter, a polka music fan. He was sure that if he got to know her better, there would be *something*, because there always was — like with Izzy, there had been lots of things.

For the next few blocks, he thought of all the things that had been wrong with Izzy. Her embarrassing laugh. Her obsessive gum chewing. Calling him goofy names that made no sense, like Winky and Weebles. Always making him explain why he did things. None of that was why he'd broken up with her — no, that had been more about making space for himself because he was suffocating. And now there was Aqua Fish Spider Girl stirring up feelings that his time with Izzy had only hinted at. He had never been in love with Izzy. It had never been as if he couldn't stop thinking about her. Was that the test? The true test of love? What *was* the test? Would he have taken a bullet for Izzy? Maybe. But not because he couldn't live without her, but because otherwise he wouldn't have been able to live with himself. That wasn't love. He didn't know what love was, not really. But he was sure that what happened inside him when he was around June was something he'd never felt before.

June sat in the car for a long time thinking. She did not need another head case in her life, and Wes . . . clearly, there was something wrong with him. She'd noticed that before with other guys. The really intense ones — the ones that were interesting — were all unstable. But she'd never met one quite like Wes, who seemed so ordinary from a distance, but then when you got closer, it was like he was burning up inside, and that made her feel as if she was burning up inside too, and she didn't need that. She really didn't need it.

Later, at home, she called Jerry back and talked to him for almost an hour. He made her laugh, and he had his own intensity. It was all about politics, but it was intense. A more comfortable, less invasive brand of intensity.

They made plans to go out Saturday night. June decided it would be okay for Jerry to see her with her black eye. It wasn't all that black anymore. More grayish yellow. But it was okay because he believed her story about hitting the doorknob with her face. Besides, Jerry did not look at her the way Wes did. When Wes looked at her she knew — she *knew* — that he was absorbing every detail. With Jerry it was more like he was seeing the *idea* of her. She could leave out one of her contacts and he would never notice. Wes had noticed right away. Those eyes of his. So hungry.

She thought she understood why he had run, but she couldn't put it into words. He ran because he had to, and —

"June?"

For half a second, June didn't know where she was. Then her bedroom came into focus and she realized that the voice had come from the phone pressed against her ear.

"Jerry," she said.

"I thought we got disconnected," he said.

"Sorry. I was just thinking about something."

"What?"

"Just stuff. What do you want to do tomorrow?"

"I don't know. A movie?"

"That would be nice." It would be easy. They would sit in the dark and watch the movie and not talk or even touch each other. She could do that. With Jerry.

EIGHTEEN

AFTER A COUPLE HOURS of laying on the old guilt trip for his violating house arrest, Wes's mom eased off, and he spent the rest of the weekend in zombie mode. He was so out of it — he'd been out of it for weeks, apparently — he was taken by surprise when his dad came home with a Christmas tree.

"Christmas? Already?"

"Duh-uh!" said Paula. "It's only like break starts on *Thursday*!" She glared at him, then added, "I got you something really nice," letting him know he had better reciprocate.

The next day, Wes obtained permission from his jailers to go to the mall. He wandered from store to store for an hour and saw lots of cool stuff that June might have liked, but he had no idea what to get his own little sister. He finally bought her a gift certificate at the bookstore. She liked to read. He would wrap it in a big box so she wouldn't know what it was. He didn't find anything for his mom and dad. He knew he wasn't thinking straight. June's face kept popping up, and he kept shoving it back, jamming it deep into the folds of his brain, stuffing the cracks with a cerebral version of black cotton fuzz, which he seemed to have in abundance.

By Monday morning, his head was packed with the stuff — the *fuzz* — and he headed for school with a muted sense of dread.

He saw Jerry almost right away.

"Hey," Wes said.

"Hey," Jerry replied.

That was pretty much it. First period, June was absent. The day passed. He got piles of makeup work in each of his classes, and lots of ribbing from the two Alans, and Calvin, and Robbie. He didn't see Izzy except once from a distance. After school he ran into Jerry again outside by the buses.

"Hey," Wes said.

Jerry nodded and gave him a tight smile.

"Look, I'm sorry," Wes said.

" 'S'all right." Jerry's shoulders relaxed.

Wes said, "So, how's the campaign going?"

"I'm taking a break until after break," Jerry said.

"Cool. So . . . how's June?" His voice did something weird. He hoped Jerry hadn't heard it.

"She's okay." He seemed suddenly eager to talk. "You know, she was sick all last week, but I saw her Saturday. Only she had to leave this morning for San Diego with her parents, some family emergency thing. They'll be gone over break. I bought her a necklace, but I guess it'll have to be a New Year's present instead of for Christmas. She texted me from San Diego. It's eighty degrees there. You want to see the necklace?"

Wes didn't, but he said, "Sure."

Jerry opened his backpack and came out with a small blue satin and felt jewelry box. He opened the box. Inside was a gold chain with a pendant made of two interlocked hearts.

Wes almost said, *Isn't that kind of corny?* But he caught himself just in time.

"Nice," he said.

"You think she'll like it?"

"Sure. Girls like that kind of stuff."

Jerry beamed pathetically and put the box back in his pack. "You taking the bus today?"

Wes looked at the metal tube filled with kids.

"It's not that cold," he said.

Knowing that June was thousands of miles away helped him relax. He did not have to think what to do next, or what not to do. He walked home letting little thoughts — fragments of memory and intention — flicker across the surface of his mind. He thought about how clean he had gotten the garage last fall, and what June would have thought if she had seen it. He thought of a clever thing he might say in language arts, and wondered if she would get it, whether she would laugh. He tried walking perfectly, making each footfall exactly the same. He caught himself smiling, and he realized that he was imagining her watching him with her aqua eyes, and that because she was so far away, he did not have to stop himself from thinking of her.

After the first hour in the air, the land changed from white to brown, a crazy quilt of earth and dead vegetation. When they flew over a city, or a large town, the homes and highways and fallow crops looked to June like an infection, out of control, sending out invasive tentacles in every direction. That was Mr. Reinhardt's fault, with his petri dishes full of mold and germs, talking about how bacteria "colonize" their medium. She liked looking at the rivers, those dark, purposeful arteries and veins, always flowing. There was a lake, and another river, and something moving swiftly across the land. A shadow. The shadow of the airplane.

She wondered if Wes had ever been on an airplane. He would like it. Not the part about being stuck in a seat for hours, but the part where places come and go so quickly.

Her parents, sitting in the two seats to her left, were talking about this and that. June heard her dad say something about Omaha, Nebraska. She leaned forward, looked past her mother, and asked, "You're going to Omaha?"

"I got a call from Omaha-Benford Bank," he said. "They have an account that's having some cash-flow problems. The bank's on the hook for about sixteen million. It's a nice gig, but things are going so well at Sani-Made, I'm thinking of staying on in Minnesota."

"The Sani-Made board of directors is talking about making your father CEO," said her mother. "A permanent position."

"You mean we wouldn't have to move again?"

"If I get the job," her dad said. "I'll know more next week. It's not a sure thing, but it's looking very positive."

"Good. I don't think I'd like Omaha."

"Oh, Junie," her mother said. "You've never even *been* to Omaha!"

"Have *you*?"

"Well, no."

Her father said, "The point is, whatever happens, we go forward. 'There Is No Reverse Gear in Time Machine.'"

"Dad! Enough with the one-way time machine already!"

Elton Edberg laughed and said, "Next!"

June sat back and stared out the window and gingerly, cautiously, delicately — as if she was performing surgery or defusing a bomb — allowed herself to think about the future.

WINTER

NINETEEN

CHRISTMAS CAME AND WENT. Wes got a sweater he liked, a shirt he hated, and a bunch of other stuff. He hung out with the two Alans a few times, lost more money at poker, went with Paula and his parents to visit various relatives, ate a lot of food, and caught up on the schoolwork he'd missed during his suspension. There were long periods of time when he didn't think about June at all. It was during one of those periods — one morning a couple of days before school started up again — that his mom called him to the phone. He figured it was Alan Hurd, trying to get him involved in another poker game, but when he picked up the phone, a small voice, very far away, said, "Hi."

Suddenly, there was no air in the room. Wes hunched over the phone, as if to keep anyone from grabbing it away from him.

"It's me," she said.

"Hi," he said.

Paula, wearing her new Christmas pajamas and eating a bowl of cereal, watched him from the kitchen table. He turned his back to her.

"Happy Almost New Year's," June said.

"Happy New Year."

"What are you doing?" she asked.

"I just had breakfast."

"What time is it there?"

"I don't know. Nine thirty, I guess."

"It's seven thirty here."

"In San Diego."

"La Jolla, actually. We came here because my aunt was dying. She died three nights ago."

"Sorry."

"She had cancer. My dad's half sister. I never really knew her. The funeral is today."

"Oh." His throat felt tight.

"We fly back tomorrow. New Year's Eve."

"Oh." Like trying to breathe through a straw.

"Do you want to do something when I get back?"

"I don't —" Wes tried to take a breath, but his chest refused to expand. "Okay," he managed to say.

June laughed. "Don't sound so eager!"

"Sorry. Um . . . when?"

"New Year's Eve?"

"Okay. What do you want to do?"

"I don't care."

"I maybe know about a couple of parties."

"I guess . . . look, let's just talk when I get back, okay?"

"Okay."

"I gotta get off the phone now."

"Okay. Bye." He clicked off, then forced himself to stand up straight and breathe.

Paula was staring at him suspiciously.

"*You* were talking to a *girl*," she said.

Wes glared at her.

Paula said, "You want to know how I know?"

"Not really." Actually, he did.

"Because you're acting all weird."

"I am not."

"Yes you are. Like your stomach hurts."

June stared at her phone. She had asked him out. He had said, "Okay." Was that okay? She would break up with Jerry when she got back. She had broken up with guys before. Besides, Jerry had his political campaign to focus on. They'd had fun, seen some movies, done some other stuff, made out a few times. . . . It wasn't like they were engaged or anything; she'd only known him four months. Not even. She could maybe do it over the phone. Would that be okay? Probably not. She had read someplace that the telephone breakup was bad. It would have to wait until she got back.

It wasn't as if she had a choice. Some things just had to happen, like two trains heading toward each other on the same track. It wasn't like you could swerve to avoid the collision. It wasn't like you could stop.

CHAPTER TWENTY

THEIR FLIGHT LANDED AT NOON on New Year's Eve, just as the snow began to fall. By the time they got home, there was half an inch on the ground. June unpacked and bathed and tried to pick out an outfit for herself, something Wes might like. Not too girly, but something that would leave him no doubt that she was a girl. In the middle of the winter in January, that was nearly impossible. She finally settled on a thick but close-fitting sweater and a pair of jeans that showed off her butt but didn't make her legs look too skinny.

Her black eye was completely gone.

She called Wes around three. He seemed nervous, and almost right away he asked her if she had talked to Jerry.

"I talked to him yesterday," she said, "from La Jolla."

"And?"

"And what?"

"Does he know we're going out?"

"I don't tell him every detail of my life."

"Yeah, but —"

"Actually, he thinks I won't be back until tomorrow."

Wes didn't say anything.

June said, "I just didn't want to deal with him on — you know — New Year's."

Wes didn't say anything, again.

"Anyway," said June, "what time are you coming over?"

Wes cleared his throat. "Eight? I know a party we could go to, but . . ."

"But what?"

"I think Jerry might be there."

"Oh."

"Maybe we can talk about it when I come over."

"Okay."

"So . . . see you later?"

"Okay."

June hung up with a sense of dread mixed with nausea. *Drausea.* Five minutes ago she had felt great, all excited to be seeing Wes again, ringing in the New Year and all that, and now suddenly she was drauseated. This was what happened whenever she got to know people, got connected to them. The only good thing was that every time her life turned to crap, she didn't have long to wait for her parents to move so she could start the cycle all over again.

Her cell phone rang. It was Jerry. June discovered a hard, cold place in herself. She answered the phone as if she had no idea who was on the line.

"Hello?"

"June! It's Jer."

"Jerry. I was just thinking about you."

"Me too. It's snowing here. What's it like in La Jolla?" Jerry always liked to talk about the weather. Politics and the weather.

"I'm here. We came home early," she said.

"Cool! So we can do New Year's together!"

June went to her hard, cold place, took a breath, and said, "Jerry . . ."

Something in her voice must have told him something.

He said, "Wait . . . June? Are you mad at me or something?"

How did clueless Jerry all of a sudden get so perceptive? She said, "No, I just think maybe we —"

"Wait! How about if I come over and we can talk? I really want to see you."

"Jerry, I don't think —"

"Wait!"

"No! Listen to me, Jerry. I can't —"

"Would you just *wait* a second?"

"I can't," June said. She really couldn't. She had to do this now. "I can't go out with you anymore."

She could hear him breathing.

Then he said, in a smallish voice she hadn't heard before, "Why?"

"Just . . . because."

The snow continued to fall, big sparkly storybook snowflakes drifting slowly from a low gray sky. By the time Wes arrived at June's, it was four inches deep. His mom had almost gone back on her promise to let him use her car, but he'd somehow convinced her that the weather wasn't that bad, and he'd promised her that he would only drive to June's, and then to Alan's party, and no place else. And of course he swore every which way not to take even a sip of alcohol.

June answered the door. "My dad said to tell you to behave yourself," she said.

Wes looked past her, expecting to see Elton Edberg's wolfish smile.

"They're not home," she said.

Wes felt the tension go out of his shoulders.

"You want to come in?"

Wes stepped up into the entryway and became weirdly conscious of his height. Not that he was tall, but he was taller than June, and now she seemed smaller than he remembered. She was holding her shoulders in and bending forward ever so slightly, making her seem even smaller, looking up at him with those eyes. She took a step back. Wes closed the door, awkward and suddenly shy.

June said, "He's not so bad, my dad."

"I didn't say anything."

"My mom says he acts like he does because he's in a business where he has to be right all the time."

"He seems like an okay guy. I mean, for a girl's dad."

June laughed.

There was another awkward moment.

"Um . . . can I get you something to drink?"

"I promised my mom I wouldn't."

"I mean, like, a glass of water."

He nodded, embarrassed. She turned quickly away and made for the kitchen. Wes stomped the snow off his feet and started to follow her, then thought better of it and toed off his sneakers. In the kitchen, June was pouring water into a glass from a dispenser on the refrigerator door. She turned toward him and sort of jumped, surprised to find him there, so close. Had she expected him to wait by the door? Why wasn't she talking? He was confused.

"Here," she said, stepping toward him. Wes reached out, but instead of handing him the glass, she moved into his arms and they were kissing, and for a moment, there was nothing in his corner of the universe but lips and tongues and her body pressing into him, and he knew in some distant fragment of his consciousness that he was falling, not falling to the floor but falling into a vortex that had opened deep inside himself as his awareness spread to every pore, as if he were lit up and glowing like a firefly, and then he heard the sound of shattering glass but he didn't stop because as long as that moment lasted, he believed to his core that it never had to end.

It was happening to June too. She was sure that what she was feeling was exactly what Wes was feeling, except that even as it was happening she sensed a jittery, anxious aura, and a tiny voice inside her — Fearful June, or perhaps Pragmatic June — was saying, *He's going to bolt. He's going to run away again.* But as the kiss went on, she banished the other Junes and let herself sink into the moment even though she knew in a distant sort of way that the panic she sensed was coming not from Wes, but from deep within herself. Then came the sound of breaking glass, and Scornful June was laughing in her ear, and she tried to pull away but her body would not let her, and then somehow she tore herself loose, gasping for breath as their arms came apart and they once again became two people, separate and distinct, but not as separate and distinct as before.

"I dropped the glass." Her voice had turned husky and deep. She looked down; Wes was in his stocking feet. Shards of wet glass were everywhere. "Careful."

Wes was staring at her stupidly, his mouth slightly open, his eyes glazed over.

"There's glass all over the floor," June heard herself say. "Don't move."

She got the sponge mop from the kitchen closet and moistened it, then started mopping, dragging the water and glass away from Wes's feet. Wes watched her silently. She could feel his eyes sending out tractor beams — even though they were separated by a few feet of space, there remained an unbreakable bond. Unbreakable? No, it was more like being connected by glass fibers — hard as steel, brittle as chalk.

"I got it all, I think." She squeezed out the mop over the sink.

Wes took a step toward her.

"Wait," she said.

He stopped.

The panicky feeling had come to the surface again, settling around her middle like her own personal lightning storm. She knew that if they kissed again, there would be no stopping. She wasn't afraid of sex — it would happen or it wouldn't. It wasn't about that. It was more that if she didn't slow it down — *way* down — there would be no place left to go.

He'd been body-slammed from the inside out. What had just *happened* here? June was standing with her back to the sink, gripping the edge of the counter so hard her knuckles were white, staring at him like she was afraid. Afraid? Had he done something wrong? He was sure she'd wanted to kiss — she'd made that perfectly clear — and they hadn't done anything more. Although it had been an amazing kiss. Izzy had never kissed him like that — like she wanted to be *inside* of him.

He said, "Hey . . ."

"I broke up with Jerry."

"Oh." Not that that explained anything.

"I called him."

"Is he . . . is he okay?"

"I guess. You know him better than me."

Did she mean he knew Jerry better than she did, or that he knew Jerry better than he knew her?

She said, "I just thought, if we go to this party —"

"We don't have to," Wes said.

"I mean, if we did go and Jerry was there, and if he still thought I was in California and his, you know, his girlfriend or something . . . it would be awful. So I had to tell him."

Wes nodded.

June said, "So who's having a party?"

"Alan Hurd."

"Which Alan is he?"

"The shorter one."

"Is it far?"

"You . . . you want to go?"

"I think we should," said June.

TWENTY-ONE

CARS LINED BOTH SIDES OF THE STREET in front of the Hurd residence; many of them had been there long enough for the snow to completely cover their windshields.

"Alan's parents are in Florida," Wes said.

"They left him home alone?"

"Supposedly his older sister Hannah is there. She's twenty-two. Except she went on an overnight and made Alan swear not to have any parties while she was gone. That was what gave him the idea."

June laughed.

"Seriously," Wes said. "They don't get along so well, and Alan knew that even if she found out, she couldn't say anything to their parents because she wasn't supposed to leave him home alone. It's a weird family."

"They're all weird," June said. "Families."

"No kidding." Wes parked at the end of the line of cars and turned to June. "It might be kind of crazy," he said.

"I could use some crazy," June said. She didn't mean it. *Crazy* she did not need, but it seemed like a funny thing to say, so she said it. Wes laughed. She liked that, his easy laugh. They were almost back to normal, or what felt like normal — a new normal. Just enjoying being together, the way people are supposed to.

"We don't have to stay long."

"I wonder if the Bitches will be there."

"Which bitches?"

"Phoebe, Britt, and Jessica."

"Oh. *Those* bitches. They'll probably be at every party in town. The question is, Which party will they be at when Phoebe passes out in somebody's parents' bedroom?"

"Really?"

"That's what happened last year."

June nodded, but she wasn't really thinking about Phoebe; she was wondering again whether Jerry would be there. She didn't think so. When they'd talked on the phone — their conversation had gone on for twenty minutes before she was able to end it — Jerry had told her he was staying home all night. He'd even made a sort of lame joke: "New Year's Eve parties are bad for politicians," he had said. "You never know when you might find yourself on YouTube."

That was actually pretty funny, she thought. *For Jerry*. Or maybe he hadn't been joking.

"You up for this?" Wes asked.

"Let's do it."

They could hear the music the moment they stepped out of the car.

"Pretty loud," Wes said. "I can guess how this party's going to end."

"With police?" said June.

"Exactly." He walked around the car and offered June his arm.

It felt right and natural. She hooked her mittened hand around his elbow and they stepped onto the sidewalk, kicking up snow as they walked, not too fast, toward the house. It was almost spooky, he thought, how he could be with June with neither of them talking, and have it feel so right. With Izzy the talking had never stopped. They were almost to the door when it opened and two guys wearing letter jackets tromped out, one of them saying in a loud voice, "This party sucks!"

Wes knew one of them, a senior named Bryan something, kind of an idiot but not a bad guy. The two lettermen lurched past Wes and June, laughing at something, and headed across the street to their car, one of them yelling, "Next!"

"I don't think I'd get in *that* car," June said.

The door was standing open. Wes and June stepped inside and found themselves tripping over a sea of shoes and boots.

"I think that's a hint," Wes said.

"I hate stocking-foot parties," June said, pulling off her boots.

The house was packed. A Foo Fighters song was tearing up the living room speakers while some bowel-thumping hip-hop filtered up from the basement. Dozens of loud voices were striving to be heard over the music. Wes didn't recognize the first ten people he looked at, which meant that Alan had long since lost control of events. Control was not Alan Hurd's strongest quality.

Wes and June threaded through the partygoers, looking for Alan. They found him holding court beside a keg planted in a huge bucket of ice in the middle of the kitchen, surrounded by a crowd of people representing every level of inebriation.

Alan's mother would have died on the spot. Wes could feel his socks sticking to the beer-sloshed tile floor. A cloud of cigarette and marijuana smoke hung in an eye-stinging haze. Something green and drippy had spattered the white cupboards.

Alan caught sight of Wes and shrieked: "Wesley Weston Westerhiemer freaking Andrews. You came!"

Every face in the kitchen turned toward him, saw who he was, then promptly lost interest — except for Jerry Preuss, who was slumped against the sink holding a cigarette in one hand and a bottle of lime vodka in the other. He was wearing somebody's bra around his neck, and his eyes were pointing in two different directions. Wes had never before seen Jerry drink or smoke, but he knew instantly that Jerry was profoundly and irredeemably polluted.

Alan shouted, "Pour my man Wes a beer!" but Wes was already backing out of the room. He turned, looking for June, but he couldn't find her. Had she left already? He stepped over some guy — Robbie Johanson, flat on his back, staring up at the ceiling fan. Wes ran to the front door, thinking June might have panicked and left. Her boots were still there. He went back through the house, checking the bedrooms. No June. He went down the stairs to the basement. Phoebe Keller and Britt Spinoza were feeding people from a salad bowl full of cherry Jell-O shots.

Back upstairs, in the kitchen, somebody told him June and

Jerry had gone out to the screen porch in back. Wes rolled open the sliding glass door and stepped through.

June was sitting on the porch swing with Jerry sprawled across her lap. June looked up at Wes and did this thing with her mouth and eyes. He understood that she was telling him to be cool. A second later he realized that Jerry was sobbing.

CHAPTER
TWENTY-TWO

"THERE'S NO WAY HE CAN GO HOME LIKE THIS." Wes had grabbed Alan from the kitchen and pulled him out onto the screen porch, where Jerry was now on his hands and knees, puking, with June standing over him helplessly.

Alan was nearly as drunk as Jerry. He said, "Wow. It's freezing out here," as if he had completely forgotten it was winter.

Wes said, "Listen, Alan, you've got to let him stay here tonight."

Alan was looking through the glass doors into the kitchen, where Calvin Warner was pouring beer directly from the tap into his mouth; half of it was running over his chin and dribbling onto the floor.

"My mom's gonna kill me," he said in a moment of sober realization.

"When does she get back?"

"Two days."

"You'll be fine," Wes said.

Jerry unleashed another cascade of lime-green vomit.

Alan looked at him and grimaced. "You think he's empty yet?"

"I wouldn't count on it," Wes said. "Here, I got his car keys. Don't let him drive."

"Whatever," Alan said, taking the keys.

June was bending over Jerry, saying something in a low voice, then helping him stand up.

Jerry looked blearily from Wes to Alan, his cheeks wet with tears and his chin wet with something else. "I'm really sorry, man." He threw one arm over June's shoulder, lurched toward Wes, and captured him with the other arm. "I love you guys. You guys are the best. I know you're gonna be, like, the happiest couple on the whole damned planet. I'm happy for you, really . . . I . . . I . . . uh-oh." He bent forward and threw up on Wes's feet.

Alan said Jerry could crash on the fold-out sofa in the basement, but at the moment it was in use by the Jell-O shot–powered hip-hop contingent. June and Wes propped Jerry in an unoccupied corner.

"You guys, you guys are the best," he kept saying. "I love you guys."

It was embarrassing.

June whispered in Wes's ear, "If I don't get out of here in about ten seconds, I'm going to start throwing up myself."

"Me too," said Wes.

They found their shoes by the front door. Wes put his sneakers on his bare feet — he'd thrown his vomit-soaked socks in the trash — and they walked out of the house into the snow.

"Wow," said June.

The flakes dropping from the sky were enormous — each one was a clump of individual flakes.

"Listen," said June. "You can hear them hit."

Wes listened. Even with the deep bass emanating from the house, they could hear the clumps of flakes landing — *chuff, chuff,*

chuff — the softest, quietest sound imaginable, multiplied tens of thousands — *millions* — of times.

"Let's walk," June said.

Being outside in the snow made June feel clean again, as if the party had been nothing more than a bad dream. She held on to Wes's arm and they walked slowly down the sidewalk, kicking through snow so light and fluffy that walking through it felt effortless. They didn't talk. It felt exotic and daring, the not talking. Especially after what had happened with Jerry, the blubbering and vomiting and everything. How could they not talk about it? But she felt no desire to revisit the events of the party. There was no need. It was like her dad always said: *Next!* It was enough to be walking side by side with Wes, holding his arm and bumping shoulders, snowflakes gently landing on their faces, sometimes perching on her eyelashes for a moment before being blinked off. She imagined stopping and piling the snow into a huge mound, then tunneling into it and huddling together in their igloo, pressing their bodies together for warmth.

"I love snow," she said, and it was true — although until that moment, she had always hated it. "I could walk like this all night."

Wes didn't say anything for a few steps, then he said, "All night?"

"Well, for a long time anyway."

"Uh . . . me too . . . except my feet are kind of cold."

"Oh!" June said, stopping. "I forgot. No socks!"

They ran the five blocks back to the car, slipping several times, but never quite falling. Once they got inside, the windows fogged up in an instant. Wes started the engine and waited for it to warm up.

June said, "I'm sorry I forgot about your feet."

"You're sorry you forgot about my feet?"

It was the funniest thing either of them had ever heard; they laughed so hard the windows got foggier, even with the defroster blasting. After they stopped laughing, June said, "Take your shoes off and give me your feet."

"Really?"

"Come on."

Wes toed off his wet sneakers and twisted awkwardly in the driver's seat to put his bare feet on her lap.

"Ew, they're all wet!" June used her mittens to dry his feet, then rubbed them with her hands.

"Your hands are hot," Wes said.

"I can't believe you walked all that way with no socks."

"It wasn't that cold, at least at first."

"You have nice feet."

"Nice, stinky feet?"

"They don't stink." She sniffed his toes, then laughed. "I mean, I've smelled worse."

They sat there without talking for a while as the car warmed up, June idly running her hands over his feet.

"Your middle name isn't really August, is it?"

"It's John. Totally boring."

"You know how I got my little scar?"

"Grizzly bear attack, right?"

"I was five. You know how moms are always yelling at you to not run with scissors? I was running with scissors. So cliché."

"Not cliché. Classic."

"Like your middle name."

They sat listening to the defroster.

Wes said, "What if nothing ever had to be different?"

"Like what?"

"Like we could just sit here forever. Take turns giving each other foot rubs. We're connected now, you know. Invisible threads."

June nodded. She knew exactly what he meant. "I think we were connected a long time ago," she said.

Wes thought back to the time they had met walking home. She was right; he had felt it even then. He said, "Do you think, like, years from now, it'll still be there?"

"The connection?"

"The connection."

June considered, then said, "I don't know." She really didn't.

"Maybe it's like a radio signal. As long as one of us is sending, we're connected."

"What about when we're asleep?"

"We connect through our dreams. Like we could be a thousand miles apart and I'd still know you were there."

June felt her heart lurch, and for a moment she imagined it — a thousand miles between them. All too real.

She said, "We could just stay here, like you said."

"We might get hungry."

"We could order a pizza."

"Do they deliver pizzas to cars?"

"Why not?"

They talked about living in a car, and other things, as the windows slowly cleared.

"Look," June said.

Wes turned his head to look out the windshield. A police car, lights flashing, had stopped in front of the party house.

"Right on schedule," Wes said.

WES LOVED DRIVING IN THE SNOW, at night, hardly any traffic, the tires squeaking softly, sliding just a little on the turns, big clumps of flakes flattening on the windshield for a moment before being swept aside by the wiper blades. They drove randomly through the neighborhoods, not talking much. Many of the houses still had their holiday lights burning.

"We're inside a snow globe," June said.

And that was what it felt like.

"You know what we need?" June asked.

At that moment, there was nothing Wes wanted more than to be driving in the snow with June by his side.

"Hot chocolate," June said, answering her own question.

Hot chocolate, to Wes, meant stirring instant cocoa into a mug of milk and heating it up in the microwave. June had something more elaborate in mind.

Standing in the kitchen, he remembered the day they'd bonked heads at the SA, the first day they'd kissed. Now, watching June, he could feel that same energy, that same force that had brought them together that day. Almost as if the air was buzzing.

"You want to get the milk out of the fridge?" she said as she placed two saucepans on the counter.

Wes opened the refrigerator and found a carton of milk. Whole milk, not skim milk like his mom always bought.

June was peeling the wrapping off an enormous bar of chocolate with some foreign name. She could feel Wes's eyes on her as she broke off a chunk and began chopping it to bits with a knife.

"You want to put a little water in the small pan?"

"How much?" Wes asked.

"Just a splash," she said. Wes was sure she could tell by the way he handled the saucepan that he wasn't used to cooking. "Put it on the stove and turn the burner to low."

Wes did so, then awaited further instructions. She told him to measure two cups of milk into the other pan. As he did that, she brought the cutting board to the stove and scraped the chopped chocolate into the pan with the water.

"I need a whisk," she said. "Top drawer, left of the sink."

Wes opened the drawer. "What's a whisk?" he asked.

June laughed. "A wire thing, like for stirring."

Wes sorted through the various kitchen tools and came up with something that looked sort of whisklike.

"That's it," June said.

As he handed her the whisk their fingers touched, and he realized that it was the first time they'd touched since she had rubbed his feet in the car. Again, he felt the force pushing him toward her, but he resisted. For the moment, thinking about it was enough.

"What next?" he asked.

"Put the milk on the stove."

Wes was beginning to feel more comfortable — he hadn't screwed up or broken anything yet. He loved the way June moved, the way she was intently whisking the chocolate, like it was the most important thing in the universe.

"You have to keep stirring," she said. "You want to pick out a couple of mugs? The cabinet next to the fridge."

This is like a dance, Wes thought as he moved past her to get the mugs, almost but not quite touching. She stopped whisking for a moment to turn up the heat under the milk, then went back to stirring.

"All these mugs have the names of companies on them," Wes said.

"Places my dad's worked. My arm's getting tired. Can you stir for a while?"

Wes took over the whisking.

"Just keep it moving," June said. "I'll get the whipped cream."

It was awkward at first, but he quickly got the hang of it and kept whisking the melting chocolate as June added dollops of warm milk. He loved that they were doing something together — not just being together, but having a goal, even if the goal was hot chocolate.

"I like the way you whisk," June said, and he felt it all up and down his spine.

They sipped their hot chocolate on the sofa in front of the flickering gas fireplace, talking about things. Later, thinking about that night, Wes could not remember what they had talked about. He did remember that when he took his first sip he got whipped cream on the tip of his nose, and June had laughed, then wiped the glob of cream off with the tip of her index finger and put it in her mouth. And he remembered the clock on the wall chiming midnight.

"It's here," June said.

Their New Year's kiss was soft as snowflakes colliding. Their lips came together lightly, and they stayed that way for so long — nothing touching but their lips — that June thought she might pass out. And then they drew apart and looked into each other's eyes, and it was magic.

Wes and June were sitting on the sofa in the living room, Wes's arm resting lightly across her shoulders, their feet propped on the coffee table — he was wearing a pair of Mr. Edberg's argyle socks, her feet were bare — when they heard her parents' car pull into the garage. Wes took his arm back and sat up straight as Mr. and Mrs. Edberg walked in the door.

Mr. Edberg saw them sitting there. He didn't say anything at first. Wes had no idea what to expect.

After a moment, Mr. Edberg said, "Happy New Year," and tried for a smile, but gave it up. Both of them looked dead tired.

"Happy New Year," said both Wes and June.

"I like your socks," June's father said.

"Thank you, sir," said Wes.

"Not going to call me El?"

"That would feel too weird, sir." Wes wasn't trying to be sarcastic; it was the simple truth.

Mr. Edberg took a moment to process that, then nodded.

"I understand," he said.

"Time to say good night to Wesley, dear," Mrs. Edberg said to June.

Mr. Edberg held up a hand. "Just because we're old and need our beauty rest doesn't mean these youngsters can't keep celebrating," he said to his wife. "It's the New Year, after all." Looking at June, he added, "Just don't break into the liquor cabinet or play any loud music, okay?"

June nodded.

A minute later, they were alone again. Wes and June stared at each other.

"That was freaky weird," June said.

CHAPTER

TWENTY-FOUR

IN THE MORNING, JUNE OPENED HER EYES feeling as if she had awakened into a new world. She looked at her clock. It was almost ten. She sat up and stretched, then went to her window and looked outside.

Fairyland. The snow had formed improbably tall caps on fence posts, birdhouses, mailboxes, and trash cans. Every twig on every tree supported a ridge of sparkling snow. The world had turned pure and white and clean.

June thought it the most beautiful thing she had ever seen. Then her mother came into her room and sat down on her bed with this awful frozen expression on her face.

Paula had gotten a new board game for Christmas. Wes had refused to play it with her, and she'd gotten really mad at him. She started doing things like not telling him about his phone messages, informing on him for every infraction of household rules, and refusing to help him fold his laundry, a task she had once undertaken with great pride. Wes, in a self-involved fog, had hardly noticed he was being dissed by his little sister, which made her even madder.

But on the morning of New Year's Day, Paula walked into the living room and found her brother lying on his stomach on the carpet playing with her new game, making designs out of the colored tiles and little men. She almost choked with indignation.

"Who said you could play with my game?!"

Wes looked up and grinned. "Nobody."

"Well, you can't!" she said.

"You don't want to play?"

"You said you didn't want to. You said it was stupid."

"I didn't mean it," Wes said.

Paula stared at him.

"Do you want to play or not?" he said.

"I have to eat breakfast."

"So eat your cereal in here."

"We're not supposed to."

"Mom's at aerobics, and Dad went to play racquetball. I won't tell, if you promise not to spill."

Paula could find no fault with Wes's offer, and a few minutes later she was sprawled on the floor with a bowl of Froot Loops, explaining the rules of the game. Wes pretended not to understand even the simplest instructions, forcing Paula to explain things over and over, which delighted her, even though she knew he was just acting stupid to tease her. They were just getting started playing a real game when the phone rang.

"I bet it's your secret girlfriend," Paula said.

Wes jumped up and checked the number on the kitchen phone. It was June. As he lifted the receiver, Paula shrieked, "Hi, Wes's Secret Girlfriend!"

Wes just laughed and closed the kitchen door and leaned back on it.

"Hey," he said into the phone. He listened, sliding slowly down the door until he was sitting on the floor. After a few more seconds, June stopped talking.

She said, "Aren't you going to say anything?"

Omaha. Three hundred fifty miles away. She might as well be moving to Neptune. In two weeks she would be moving to Neptune.

Sani-Made, after all their talk about hiring her dad permanently, had decided not to renew his contract. In fact, they had fired him. On New Year's Eve, just as he was leaving work.

It wasn't the first time her dad had been let go suddenly. In the workout business, getting axed was almost normal. The company owners let him come in and do the dirty work, and then turned around and did the same thing to him.

Her dad shrugged it off. *"Next!"* He'd accepted the Omaha job twenty minutes after getting fired by Sani-Made. In fact, he was driving down the next day, leaving the task of packing up and moving to June and her mother.

"Omaha-Benford Bank has a house for us," he said. "One of their foreclosures. It's in a nice neighborhood. You'll like it."

Like it? They'd never lived anyplace long enough for her to like it. June knew better than to argue. Her father's business migrations were a force of nature — the universe conspiring to seek out every scintilla of happiness inside her and rip it out, bloody roots and all, and turn her life to a stinking pile of crap. That was what it was about. He could have gone on to his new job all by himself, let her and her mom stay in Minnesota until the end of the school year, at least — but no, he had to have the family together, as if a few months apart would somehow damage them. Damage? How could they be any more damaged than they were already?

Still, that was what scared her, what kept her in line. If she threw a screaming fit and refused to leave, what would happen? Would her family shatter? Sometimes it felt that way — one wrong move and everything would fly apart.

She spent most of the day in her bedroom making piles of stuff. Stuff to keep, stuff to give away, stuff to throw away, stuff she hadn't decided about. The throwaway pile was biggest. It included all her schoolwork, clothes from last summer, old magazines, empty and almost empty makeup containers. The downstairs phone rang. June stopped what she was doing and listened. She heard her mom's voice, a short conversation that she couldn't quite make out, then her mom coming up the stairs. She concentrated on making a perfect stack of folded T-shirts. Her mom looked in through her bedroom doorway.

"What are you doing?" she asked.

"Making piles," said June.

Her mom sat down on the bed. "That was Wesley again," she said.

"I thought it might be," June said. She had turned her cell off after talking to Wes that morning.

"I told him you weren't feeling well, and that you couldn't talk to him."

June nodded.

"I'm sorry. He seems like a nice young man."

"He is." June spoke in a voice so small she could hardly hear herself.

TWENTY-FIVE

SCHOOL STARTED AGAIN THE NEXT DAY. June was absent. Wes ran into Jerry Preuss after English class.

"Hey," Wes said cautiously.

Jerry nodded, his expression giving nothing away.

Wes said, "How are you doing?"

"I'm great," said Jerry.

"That was some crazy party," Wes said. When Jerry gave him a blank look, he added, "At Alan's? Alan Hurd?"

"Oh," said Jerry. "I don't remember much."

"I heard the cops broke it up early."

"Did they?" Jerry said.

"I think so." Wes wondered if Jerry really didn't remember, or if he was just pretending not to because he was embarrassed. It didn't really matter.

Wes said, "The Edbergs are moving."

"I know," Jerry said.

"You know?"

"She called me last night."

"She did? You talked to her?"

"I just said I did," Jerry said, half smiling, a flicker of surprise — and triumph — in his eyes. "They're going to Omaha. So what?"

"So nothing." Wes walked away, feeling more than a little sick inside.

It didn't take much for June to convince her mom that there was no point in her going back to school for one short week.

"If I stay home, I can help you with the packing," she said. "If I go to school now, we'll just start a bunch of stuff that I'll never be able to finish. Besides, I think it's best to just move on. You know. *Next!*"

Her mom laughed at that. "You've got more of your father in you than I thought," she said.

June went to work on her father's closet, packing his suits and jackets and shirts and trousers in cardboard wardrobe boxes left over from their last move. All of his suits were either navy blue or gray. *People who wear brown and green suits are perceived as untrustworthy*, he had once told her. Another one of her dad's peculiar notions.

June didn't think she was like her dad at all. But some of his ideas were hard to argue with. For example, there really *was* no reverse gear — she couldn't go back and have New Year's Eve over and over again.

How could something so inevitable be so hard? She wished she could close her eyes, turn around three times, and be there. Wherever. Not here.

Poor Wes. She felt awful for him, she really did, but she was doing him a favor really, just chopping it off, ending it, avoiding that long, awkward, painful good-bye. She should have stuck with Jerry. It was easy to say good-bye to Jerry. *Good-bye, Jerry. Have a nice life. Good luck with your political ambitions. I hope nobody at that party YouTubed you.*

So easy.

But not Wes. Thinking about not seeing him was unbearable, but not as unbearable as thinking about seeing him again, and then having to let go. Three hundred fifty miles. It wasn't really as far as Neptune. They could bridge the distance, texting and talking and sending pictures back and forth . . . but it would be only a matter of months before her dad took a job in Alaska or Alabama, or Wes would meet somebody else, or go back to that girl Izzy.

June squeezed one more sport coat into the wardrobe box. She used a fat blue marker to write *Dad's Closet* on the side and taped it up. She had done this before. All of her father's stuff would fit in seven boxes, three big and four medium. June could fit her stuff in one big box, two medium, and three small. Her life: one big, two medium, three small. There was no point in accumulating stuff if you had to move every few months. No point in accumulating anything. Friends, for example.

June went to her bedroom, back to her piles. One pile was socks. She sat down and started pairing them up. Because if she was missing one sock, there was no point in moving its mate to Omaha.

Wes would laugh at that. Or he would say, "Yeah, but what if later on you find the missing sock in a pant leg or folded up in a towel or something? Then you'd wish you still had the one you threw away." Or maybe he would say, "What's the deal with matching socks? Who says they have to match? Wouldn't the world be more interesting if people wore a different sock on each foot?" Or he might say, "You shouldn't throw it away. You should donate it to the One-legged League." And she would say, "Or the One-footed Family." And he would stick his hand in the sock like it was a puppet and say, "No! No! Pleeeeeease don't throw me away!" They would laugh.

Where was she getting this stuff? Anyway, it was a miracle: She wasn't missing any socks.

Next?

Her cell rang. She checked the number; it was Wes. She let it go to voice mail, jammed the paired socks into a shoe box, and put the shoe box in a moving carton. She dialed her voice mail and listened to his message. Same as before. He wanted to talk to her. He didn't get it. He didn't get that there was no point. That it was over. That it had never started, not really. She felt herself getting angry, and went with it. Anger was cleansing; it felt good to get mad. She thumbed an angry text into her phone and sent it quick, before she could change her mind.

Wes read the message over and over, like touching a sore.

i dont want to see u its over STOP
CALLING ME goodbye im sorry

Maybe her parents had forced her to write the message. Maybe they'd written it themselves. Maybe she was being held prisoner, or she was drugged. Because it was impossible that she didn't want to see him. It was too cruel, too insane, too . . . impossible.

But he knew it was true.

CHAPTER TWENTY-SIX

Wes stood outside June's house for what seemed like an hour, though it was probably more like ten minutes. She was in there; he could feel her presence.

He thought through the likely scenarios. June would answer the door. Or her mother. Or Mr. Edberg. Or no one would answer the door. Every one of those possibilities frightened him. He might have stood there longer, but the cold was getting to him; he walked up the unshoveled walk to the front door and rang the bell.

Mrs. Edberg opened the door and gave him this pitying look that made him want to shrivel and die.

"Wesley," she said with a sad smile.

"I really need to talk to June," Wes said. He knew he sounded pathetic.

Mrs. Edberg was shaking her head. "She can't see you right now. She's . . . busy."

"I won't stay long," Wes said. "I just need to see her."

"I'm sorry."

"I tried calling."

Mrs. Edberg nodded as he spoke. "I'm sure she got your messages. But this is not a good time."

"When would be a good time?"

Mrs. Edberg sighed. "I'm sorry, Wesley. I'm going to have to ask you to leave now."

"I'm not leaving," Wes said. "I'll wait here until she comes out to talk to me."

Mrs. Edberg's expression went from pitying to hard. "I'm afraid you'll have a very long wait." She closed the door.

Wes didn't know what to do. He could hardly believe he had said what he'd said. Refusing to leave. June clearly wanted nothing to do with him. But maybe she did, or at least if he had a chance to talk to her he could find out why she wouldn't talk to him, why she was being so mean. He kicked the snow away from the top step and sat down, his back to the door. He would sit there until June came out, or the police hauled him away, or until his butt froze to the step.

Looking out her bedroom window, June could see Wes's feet sticking out. He was just sitting there on the steps. She hoped he was wearing dry socks — it was cold out. She wished he would leave, but at the same time she loved that he wouldn't.

"Junie?" Her mother was standing in the bedroom doorway. "Are you going to let that poor boy sit out there all afternoon?"

June looked at her mother. "I'm just doing what you always say. Ending it. Not looking back."

"Go talk to him," her mother said.

"I already texted him that I didn't want to see him anymore."

"He needs to hear it from the real you."

When Wes heard the door open behind him, his entire body went rigid. He knew without looking that it was June. She sat down next to him. He kept his eyes on the street.

She didn't say anything, and after a while he turned his head, his neck bones grinding like a rusty hinge. June was wearing slippers, jeans, an enormous down jacket, and that pink cap with the long tassel. The tassel was clean. Her hands were buried in the jacket pockets. The only part of her he could see was her face from her eyebrows down to her chin. He stared hard, trying to memorize every surface, every pore, the texture of her lips, the color of her eyes. She wasn't wearing her contacts. He liked the natural color of her irises better — the pale blue, not the swimming pool aqua.

Her face was very still, as if she was asleep with her eyes open, yet still excruciatingly aware. He knew she could feel his eyes on her face. It was almost like touching her. No, it was *exactly* like touching her. He could feel his heart pumping. He could feel his skin. He could smell her, that clean, sweet smell — what had he thought before? Maple syrup and fresh-turned earth? That was not quite right. Not even close. More like pine trees and burnt sugar. And it wasn't an actual smell, not really, but the things that came into his head when he was near her.

"Stop it," she said.

"Stop what?"

"Stop looking at me."

Wes looked away, closed his eyes, and examined the fresh memory of her face.

She said, "Look, I'm sorry about that message I sent."

She said, "I just have to go on with my sucky life."

She said, "And not look back."

She said, "You know?"

She said, "Because it would be too hard."

She said, "Okay?"

Wes opened his eyes and looked at her. She was staring hard at him, her pupils drawn down to pinpricks, her face mostly pale but with red spots on her cheeks, her mouth — her lips — tight as two hard-stretched rubber bands. She looked as if she was about to crumble.

"I just wanted to see you," he said.

CHAPTER
TWENTY-SEVEN

JUNE STARED STRAIGHT AHEAD through the windshield at the moving van six car-lengths in front of them. Her mother, driving the BMW, had finally stopped talking. Four more hours to Omaha, their next destination. June put her bare feet on the dash and rested her chin on her knees. The vibration of the tires on the road traveled up her shins to her skull.

"Why are you sitting like that?" her mother asked.

"I don't know," June said.

"You should do your toenails," her mother said.

"It's winter. Who's going to see them?"

"I, for one, can see them perfectly."

June put her feet down and put in her earphones and put on some Queens of the Stone Age.

Pound my ears, she thought.

New school.

New friends.

New boyfriend.

Figure out what was what.

Who was who.

She was good at it. She thought how quickly she had found her place at Wellstone, how she had met Wes Andrews, and how much fun they'd had.

For, like, five minutes. Until her parents had sensed that she might be happy for once.

Her mother was talking again. June pulled out her left earbud.

"What?"

"I said the house has a pool."

"An *indoor* pool?"

"Outdoor. But we should be swimming in a few months."

"If we still live there. Dad will probably move us to Uzbekistan."

"Your father . . ."

"My father *what*?"

Her mother gave her a look, began to say something, then thought better of it and pressed her lips closed and shook her head and returned her attention to the road. After a few seconds she spoke again.

"This has been very hard for him."

June made a *phtt* sound with her lips.

"He *needs* this," said her mother.

"He doesn't *need* anybody."

"You're wrong. He needs *us*. He's . . . you know, just because your father and I are adults doesn't mean we're not scared shitless half the time."

June gaped at her mother, shocked. She'd never heard her talk like that before.

Her mother's face hardened. "We should be able to stay in Nebraska until you finish high school, maybe longer. I have a good feeling about this one, Junie. I —"

Junie replaced her earbud and turned up the volume, letting the relentless beat hammer smooth her thoughts. She closed her eyes. Images flickered across the screen in her brain. Wes looking at her — he had looked at her a lot, and when she looked back at him everything had become solid and real, as if the wisps of consciousness that made her who she was had congealed into something resembling a soul.

A sharp sensation, almost painful, but not quite.

"— too loud!" Her mother had yanked out her left earbud. "You'll fry your eardrums!"

June turned off the music and removed the other earbud without saying anything.

"You and all your plugged-in friends will be deaf before you're forty."

"I have no friends," June said quietly.

"You make friends as easily as your father. What's the matter with you?"

"Nothing."

Neither of them spoke for a long time, which was fine with June. She put her feet back on the dashboard and tried to remember the names of all her boyfriends. Adam, ninth grade, Olathe, Kansas — he was the cutest. The next one had been at that school in Elgin. She could almost see his face, but she couldn't remember his name. Something with a *J*. Not Jason. Not James. Not John. He was tall, she remembered. Taller than Wes.

Would she forget Wes? The thought of him disappearing from her mind caused her heart to speed up. She squeezed her eyes shut; his face swam into view: soft brown eyes, crooked, questioning eyebrows, the way he bit his lower lip when he was thinking. She had trouble with his ears — she couldn't remember his ears. Was she forgetting him already? Something in her chest crumbled. She should have taken a photo. All the times they'd been together and she'd had her cell with her, she could have taken his picture anytime. She could be looking at his ears right now.

The seat belt was too tight across her chest; she could hardly breathe.

It occurred to her to open the door and throw herself out of the car. She imagined an instant of wind filling her lungs, then the rough asphalt tearing the skin from her body. She clutched the armrest, afraid for a moment that she would actually do it.

The moment passed. She drew a deep breath, then another.

"Are you okay?" her mother asked.

"I'm hot."

"So turn down the heat."

June stared at the controls on the dash but could make no sense of them. Her mother reached out and adjusted a knob.

"Are you sure you're okay?"

June nodded. Each inhalation required an act of will. She was sure that if she stopped paying attention to her breathing, she would die.

"There's bottled water in the cooler."

June shook her head and gripped the armrest and watched the front end of the car eat up the white lines on the road as she forced the air in and out of her lungs.

In and out.

She sank into the vibrations and the sound of the wind and the tires and the rasp of air moving in and out of her body and waited for something to happen. A tire to blow, a bird to strike the windshield, an engine hose to break, a meteor to fall from the sky, a hydrogen bomb, Armageddon, the Big Crunch.

"June?" Her mother's voice.

June tried to shut her out, but ears do not close.

"Junie . . . are you crying?"

TWENTY-EIGHT

WES WAS OKAY.

He *would be* okay.

He was *going to be* okay.

There were things to do, and he did them. Wake up. Take a shower. Go to school. Go through the motions of getting an education.

He tried calling. Her cell number was no longer in service.

His parents, sensing some dark and mysterious adolescent funk, treated him as if he were made of nitrogylcerin. For a few days, Paula made a big show of pretending he didn't exist, but when he didn't seem to notice — although he really did — she began to observe him intently. He would feel her eyes following him, the way she might keep an eye on a large, scary dog.

At school, he zombied his way through his classes. He could almost hear the air hissing out of his grade point average.

Alan Schwartz had taken a cell phone photo of Jerry Preuss at the party — wasted, with the bra hanging around his neck — and printed it out with the words *Jerry Preuss for President*. The image got passed around school, but instead of destroying Jerry's political ambitions, it made him more popular. He started going out with Naomi Liddell. Naomi, it turned out, was a tireless and effective campaign worker, and she worshipped him.

Everybody she approached promised to vote for him, if only to get her to shut up and go away. Jerry seemed to enjoy her constant chatter.

The weather turned impossibly colder, with daytime highs in the single digits. Alan Hurd's parents took his car away because of the party, so Wes didn't ride with him to school anymore, but even on the coldest days he wouldn't take the bus. He did a lot of walking.

Izzy broke up with Thom Samples, and that made Wes feel better for about one tenth of a second, and then it made him feel worse.

Phoebe Keller and Josh Sandstrom had a fight and ended their relationship. Over the next couple of weeks, Wes noticed that he kept running into Phoebe at school — she kept trying to talk to him, even though she seemed to have nothing to say. Eventually, he figured out she was flirting with him. After a few days she gave up.

One Saturday, Calvin Warner, who wasn't even that good of a friend, stopped by the house and practically dragged him out of his bedroom.

"You gotta get out," he said.

"Out where?" Wes asked.

"Come on."

"I don't want to play poker."

"Screw poker. We're going to the mall. Shopping."

"Shopping for what?"

"Girls."

Wes decided it would be easier to go than to argue.

At the food court, they bought giant frozen drinks, which Calvin spiked with miniature airplane bottles of vodka he had stolen from his father's collection. They found a good place to sit in the central atrium. They sipped their drinks and waited.

"This is the best place in the world to meet girls," Calvin said. "Maybe we'll get lucky."

Wes did not say what he was thinking, which was that as far as he knew, Calvin had never had any luck with any girl, ever. Also, it was too cold for serious girl watching. Not cold inside the mall, but below zero outside, so all the girls — not that there were that many — had on so many layers of clothing that they looked like puffy jackets with legs.

He thought about saying that. *Puffy jackets with legs.* June would have laughed, but Calvin wouldn't get it. Every time he came up with something to say, Wes would feel his lips part, a seal breaking, and he would feel his breath moving out of his lungs, over his tongue, but whatever part of his larynx or brain or whatever it was that made words appear from rushing air would not engage, and instead of words he could produce only sighs.

"Check it out," Calvin said, pointing at a girl walking out of Abercrombie & Fitch.

Wes opened his mouth to say *She's, like, ten years old, you pervert.* But instead he released another sigh.

Calvin gave him a sharp look, a wordless *Dude!*

Wes leaned back on the bench, let his arms flop out to the sides, and stared up at the glass dome two stories above them. The sky was icy blue.

Calvin said, "Dude, you are seriously messed up."

The corners of Wes's mouth twitched.

"You got to, like, move on."

Wes rolled his eyes in Calvin's direction, asking for something but not knowing what.

"That June was toxic," Calvin said. "She planted some, like, alien worm inside you."

Wes heard what Calvin was saying. He had been thinking of himself with a big hole inside, but now he could feel the worm, the toxic alien worm, a long ropy thing anchored to his spine, gripping his organs with its ridges and prongs, secreting acids, belching clouds of noxious gases, gnawing on his liver. He imagined reaching in through the skin and grabbing it and ripping it out — was this what drove samurai to perform seppuku? No, samurai did not kill themselves over women; they did it for pride, to save face. Their worm was the worm of shame, but Wes guessed it felt pretty much the same.

He closed his eyes. His hand drifted to his belly, his middle finger found the indentation of his navel through his shirt; he pressed in until it hurt. If he had talons instead of fingernails he could unzip his abdomen with a single violent spasm, spill his guts onto the tile floor, detach the thing that was eating his liver, and cast it far away.

Calvin's voice came from far away. "Dude, are you okay?"

Wes managed to nod his head, a silent lie.

"What you got to do, you gotta forget about her," Calvin said. He looked around, took another mini-bottle from his jacket pocket, and poured it into Wes's drink. "You gotta *delete* her."

Wes nodded, tipped his head back to look up at the blue sky, and closed his eyes. Sooner or later he would be okay. Eventually he would be able to go hours, days even, without knowing she was there, without seeing her face.

After a time — five minutes? Half an hour? — Calvin said, "You know, you're piss-poor company lately."

CHAPTER
TWENTY-NINE

THE NEW HOUSE HAD A HUGE ENTERTAINMENT ROOM and the empty pool in the backyard. It was still too cold to swim, but if they stayed through the summer it would be great. Her new school — Hills High School — was new and clean and everybody seemed really nice. June found that most of the time she was able to stay focused on moving forward, into the future. During the day she didn't think about Wes, unless she saw somebody who looked like him, or heard a laugh that sounded like his.

At night, every night, just before she went to sleep, she would carefully dial his number on the new cell phone her mom had bought her. She let her finger rest lightly on the SEND button. She would close her eyes and see his face, almost as if she had a miniature model of Wes in her head. Some nights she thought she could feel his presence in a ghostly, distant sort of way. Was that the connection? The unbreakable connection?

Maybe it was all a game. That's what her dad would say.

But it wasn't a game. If she pressed that button, it would be real. If she pressed the button, Wes would answer. He would say, "Hey, I've been waiting for you to call."

She would say, "I know."

And they would laugh, even though it wasn't funny.

She thought a lot about what her mother had said that day in the car, about being scared shitless half the time. Scared shitless?

Was that what kept her from pressing SEND? Was that what she wanted her life to be like?

One day in February, Wes woke up to see water dripping from the eaves. A warm front had moved in overnight. He got dressed and went downstairs. Paula, always an early riser, was sitting at the counter in her pajamas, eating a bowl of cereal. She watched wordlessly as he took the orange juice from the refrigerator and drank straight from the carton. He grabbed a muffin from the bread drawer and sat down across from Paula, feeling her eyes on him. He noticed several cards and envelopes next to her.

"What's that?" he asked.

"I'm giving valentines to my seven best friends," Paula said. "It's Valentine's Day, you know."

Wes had not known that.

"You should send one to your girlfriend," Paula said.

"I don't have a girlfriend."

"I bet she'll call you," Paula said. She went back to eating her Froot Loops.

For the rest of the day, Wes kept hearing Paula's words. There were times when he thought his little sister was psychic, the way she could pull words right out of his head. Because he'd caught himself thinking that, thinking the phone would ring and he would answer it, and June's voice would come over the line into his ear. It was stupid, he knew. Stupid to think that way. But he thought it a lot, and every time the phone rang he imagined it was her. His heart would speed up, and he would listen when his mom or Paula answered it. Just in case. But it was never for him.

That night, after dinner, Wes retired to his room as usual,

muttering something about homework, but instead of doing his homework he spent the night reading old X-Men comics. The mutant telepath Emma Frost reminded him of June, especially her eyes. And the telepathy.

At ten o'clock, still without having looked at his homework, Wes was lying on his bed staring up at the faint brown splotch on his ceiling. It had been there for five years. He and Jerry had been in his room playing video games. They'd been sharing a bottle of Pepsi, and then — he couldn't remember why — he'd shaken up the bottle, holding his thumb over the top, and had tried to spray Jerry. Jerry had knocked his arm up and the cola had squirted all over the ceiling.

He remembered his mother shaking her head and saying, "Well, you're the one who's going to have to look at it for the next seven years." He looked at it all the time.

The telephone rang. Wes listened as his mother answered it from the kitchen.

A few seconds later, he heard her calling his name.

Wes allowed himself to imagine it was June, then he imagined it wasn't. Probably one of his idiot friends. He rolled off the bed and walked down the stairs. The phone was sitting on the counter, face up. He put the phone to his ear.

"Hello?"

There was the sound of distance, a breath, and then he heard her voice.

"It's me."

SPRING

THIRTY

From: Wes

I am bowling. Bored.

Mar 20 19:39

"Wes! Your turn!"

Wes looked up from his phone and blinked at the three expectant faces: Calvin and the two Alans.

"We need a strike," said Calvin. Wes and Calvin were teamed up against Alan Hurd and Alan Schwartz. They were on the seventh frame, ten dollars riding on the outcome. Wes pocketed his phone, picked up his bowling ball, and faced the pins. On either side of him, balls were rolling, pins were crashing, lights were blinking.

What am I doing? he wondered. *How did I get here?* The sixteen-pound black, battered sphere felt utterly foreign, as if he had never held such a thing in his entire life.

He slipped his fingers into the holes.

"Don't choke," said Alan Hurd as he stuffed a pretzel into his mouth.

"Shut *up*!" Calvin said. Then, to Wes, "*Focus,* dude."

Wes tried to focus. He held the ball up to his chin and stared past it down the narrow wooden lane at the ten pins. He imagined the ball sliding into the pocket, the pins exploding, the satisfying clatter of a perfect strike.

"Choke!" Alan yelled.

Wes leaned toward the alley and let the momentum carry him forward. His right arm swung back, then swung forward, releasing the ball.

His thumb stuck in the hole. The ball came off with an audible pop, arced through the air, and landed hard about ten feet down the alley.

Calvin moaned. *"Dude!"*

The ball rolled lazily toward the pins, curved to the left, dropped into the gutter.

Wes turned back to his friends. Alan Hurd was laughing, spraying pulverized pretzel all over the scoring screen. Alan Schwartz shoved him off his chair. Still laughing, Alan Hurd inhaled some pretzel and started coughing. Calvin handed him his Coke; Alan took a huge swig, then gasped and clutched his throat.

"What *is* that stuff?" he asked.

"Half whiskrumka, half Coke," said Calvin. He had raided his dad's liquor cabinet and brought a flask containing what he called a "medley of spirits": whiskey, rum, and vodka. "Nectar of the gods," he said.

"More like crotch sweat of the gods," Alan Hurd said.

"Crotch nectar!" said Calvin.

Alan Schwartz wiped the spit and crumbs off the screen with his sleeve and said to Wes, "You need a spare."

Wes regarded his friends curiously. The bright fluorescent lights made them look pale and two-dimensional. He wondered if he looked the same to them. He picked up his ball and turned to the long, narrow lane. The ten pins, a toothy V-shaped smile, mocked him. *Oh, well,* he thought, *the sooner I get this over with, the sooner it will be over.*

The ball left his hand and kissed the polished wood surface, describing a shallow, precise curve as it spun down the lane to cut into the sweet spot between the one and the three. Pins flew. For a moment he thought he'd knocked them all down, but the two corner pins — the seven and the ten — remained standing on opposite sides of the lane. After a couple of seconds, the metal arm clunked down and swept them both away.

Sometimes June pretended that Wes was her imaginary boyfriend. She would turn off her phone and put it in her purse, shut down her computer, and tell herself that she had lived her whole entire life in Omaha, and all the other places she remembered were dreams, or delusions from a psychotic past. Her dad might have called it "living in the present." Except he would be more likely to tell her that the present was an illusion, and that only the future was real.

For Christmas her dad had given her a ceiling alarm clock, so she could lie in the dark, staring at the wiggly red numbers projected onto the textured ceiling.

10:16

10:17

10:18

It made for some long nights. But it perfectly suited her father's philosophy: *The past is gone. Tempus fugit. Next!*

She tried to imagine her imaginary boyfriend Wes in a bowling alley. Were there girls there? Of course there were girls. It was a bowling alley — skank heaven. But, if there were girls, would her imaginary boyfriend have texted her?

10:22

She really needed to hear his voice. Too bad it would only be an imaginary voice. She'd maxed out the minutes on her cell, and only two-thirds of the way through the month. Good thing she had unlimited texting.

Good thing he's "imaginary," said Sarcastic June. Or maybe that was Scornful June. Or some other June.

10:25

10:25

10:25

Some minutes lasted longer than others.

THIRTY-ONE

From: JKE

**im touch tezting u by feell in histoer y
class. I cd b s pended!**

Mar 21 11:05

Wes shut off his cell and put it in the lower side pocket of his cargo pants, where it would knock against his knee with every step. He liked the reminder that it was there. He moved into the flow of students entering the school and made his way down the hall to Ms. Blum's English class.

Ms. Blum was one of those teachers who liked everybody to sit in the same seat all the time. That was fine with Wes. It saved him having to make a decision every morning at ten minutes to eight, when he was hardly awake. But when June had gone to Omaha, that left an empty desk right in the middle of the room, and Ms. Blum had asked Phoebe Keller to move there.

Now, about ten times a day, Wes felt his eyes drawn to that desk, but instead of June, he found Phoebe. What made it worse was that sometimes she caught him looking at her, and since he had ignored her obvious flirting in the weeks following June's move, she returned his confused glance with a haughty sneer. The first few times that had happened, he'd blushed, but after a while they both got used to it. Her sneer became automatic, while Wes simply looked away and went back to his thoughts.

He had told no one at school that he was staying in touch with June. It was too complicated.

One day June had been talking in the hall with Trish and Tara and Tabitha when Tabitha turned to her and said, "You're like the fourth musketeer."

June said, "Huh?"

"We're the Three Ts and you're like the fourth one. What was his name?"

"D'Artagnan?" June said.

"Yeah, him."

That was when it hit her that she had found a social circle that exactly duplicated the one she'd left behind in Minnesota. There was a guy named Cary who was a lot like Jerry Preuss — very serious and ambitious, and sort of into her. She'd made it clear to him that she already had a boyfriend, but she still noticed him looking at her a lot. There was even a geeky chatterbox named Jocelyn — a near clone of Naomi — who had glommed onto June her first week at Hills.

But no Wes clone. That would have been too incredibly weird.

"Did D'Artagnan have a first name?" Tara said.

"I'm not D'Artagnan," said June.

"How about we call you Dart?" Tabitha said. "Dart and the Three Ts."

"Sounds like an oldie rock band," said Trish.

It didn't stick. The nickname. Dart. It was stupid anyway. Back in Illinois, June had gone out a few times with an irritating guy who'd called her Junebug. She preferred her real name. Even if it was the name of a month.

At Wellstone, getting caught texting — even at lunch or between classes — meant having your phone confiscated. June said it was even worse at her new school, where texting during class could get you kicked out for a week. That didn't stop her from sending the occasional stealth text, but Wes decided to leave his phone off during school rather than chance it. In some ways it made the days go easier, but at the same time it drove him crazy. He would get a feeling, like ESP, that June was texting him at that moment, and it was all he could do to not turn on his cell and check.

The ban on cells was a huge deal for a lot of students. Even some parents, who felt they needed to be able to call their kid at any time for any reason, objected to it. There were school board meetings and articles in the student paper. A local radio station had devoted an hour to the topic, with callers from both sides of the issue. But the principal remained adamant. Absolutely No Cell Phone Use During School Hours.

Jerry Preuss had made it his number one campaign issue. He even devised a plan he called Civil Cell Disobedience. Half the students with a cell would call the other half at the exact same time, so that phones around the school would ring at once. He spent a week organizing the protest, but on the day of the event, most of the students chickened out, so only a small number of phones actually rang. Two dozen phones were confiscated.

The students who had lost their phones got mad at the gutless majority, while the gutless majority congratulated themselves on dodging a bullet. Wes would probably have lost his cell too, but he'd forgotten all about the protest and hadn't turned it on. It wasn't as if Jerry had asked Wes personally. They didn't talk much anymore.

Mostly, Wes hung out with the two Alans now, and sometimes Calvin and Robbie — as long as they were doing something that didn't cost him any money, because after paying his phone bill, every dollar he was able to get his hands on went toward financing The Plan.

The Plan: Buy a motorcycle and head for Omaha the first day of summer break.

Wes had taken a part-time job at Jamba Juice. Seven-fifty an hour, sixteen hours a week. That came to about ninety bucks a week after taxes. He had savings of another $390. By the time school let out, he would have enough to buy Calvin's cousin's old dirt bike. It wasn't really made for highway travel, but it was street legal. Gas wouldn't cost much. He hadn't checked into the insurance. He would have to learn to ride, but that shouldn't take more than a day or two — he had already passed the written test.

The hardest part would be selling The Plan to his parents. A solo motorcycle trip was probably not what they had in mind for him this summer. And even if he could talk them into it, there was the parent problem at the other end — Mr. and Mrs. Edberg might not respond well to him showing up at their front door.

Also, he hadn't yet told June what he planned to do.

His idea was to let her know on April first, when his cell minutes recharged. He would say, "I'm buying a motorcycle and driving it to Omaha." Then she would say, "Great!"

Or maybe she would say, "Are you completely insane?" In that case, he would say "April Fool!"

But when April came, they talked about other things. Anything, just to hear her voice. Like what music they were listening to. Or moving to New York City or a tropical island. Or she would talk about her new friends in Omaha, and he would tell her about people she knew, like how Jerry had all of a sudden become popular after getting drunk at Alan's party.

"How's his campaign going?" June asked.

"Naomi is his campaign manager."

He thought she would think that was funny, but all she said was, "I bet she'll do a good job."

Somehow they burned through all their cell minutes in less than a week, and he never got around to telling her about The Plan.

THIRTY-TWO

From: Wes

Its official. Jerry Preuss is our new class prez.

Apr 19 15:38

June tried not to think about the in-between future.

The *immediate* future, that was easy. It was about getting through the week. And the *distant* future — things she'd dreamed about when she was a little kid — being an astronaut, living on her own island, becoming a movie star . . . that imaginary future was fun to think about. She could make it anything she wanted. Like Jerry Preuss becoming President of the Universe.

But the *in-between* future — a month, a year, two years — she tried to shove to the back of her mind. Because it was way too fuzzy and scary.

She tried not to think about it, but her mind betrayed her several times a day. And every scenario she came up with came to a crashing, utterly impractical end. If she tried to run off with Wes, her parents would call out the National Guard, or worse. And she didn't think any of her Minnesota girlfriends would agree to put her up for the summer. As for Wes moving to Omaha . . . she could just imagine what her dad would say.

"Are you okay?"

June looked toward the voice. A boy — tall, rail thin, tousled black hair, honey-color eyes — was giving her a concerned look. They were standing in front of her open locker. The final bell had gone off a few minutes earlier. The hallway was crowded with a stampede of students heading for the exits.

"I'm fine," she said. "Why?"

"You looked upset," the boy said.

"Not really."

"Oh. Sorry." He smiled. One crooked tooth, the rest nice. "I'm Kel," he said. "Are you new?"

"I've been here since January."

"Oh." He shrugged the way boys do when they are trying to say, "Sorry," but they really aren't.

"I'm June." She had seen him around. Not actually *looked* at him, but noticed him in a peripheral sort of way because of his above-average height and supernaturally black hair. Dye job? Probably. His black T-shirt was printed with the words *Alien Sex Fiend* beneath a nail-pierced skull and crossbones. A band? It looked goth. She saw no piercings or tats, but that didn't mean anything — he might have an anarchy sign tattooed on his butt.

"Nice to meet you," said Kel. "Are you going out the front?"

For a second, June didn't get what he was asking. *Going out the front?* Then she realized he was asking her which school exit she was planning to use.

"West side," she said, pointing in the opposite direction.

"Oh, well, see ya!" Kel headed off toward the front foyer. He had a loose, long-strided way of walking that looked graceful even in those thick-soled motorcycle boots. June watched until he was out of sight, then set about rearranging the contents of her locker as the hallway slowly emptied. She took her time. Because she had lied. Because she planned to leave by the front, and she didn't want to run into Alien Sex Fiend Kel.

It was never a good idea to get to know anybody too interesting.

You'll just miss them when you leave, said Pragmatic June.

"Like Wes," June whispered.

Your preposterous fantasy lover, said Sarcastic June.

"Shut *up*!" June slammed the locker door.

"Whoa there! Don't blame it on the hardware."

June whirled to tell off whoever it was — but it turned out to be the custodian, pushing his six-foot-wide broom down the hallway.

"Contrary to what you kids think, these lockers are not unbreakable," he said.

"Sorry," June said.

The janitor nodded, satisfied, and continued pushing his broom down the hall. June slung her bag over her shoulder and followed him toward the front entrance.

> From: Wes
>
> **Im thinking about becoming a professional poker player**
>
> Apr 23 17:10

In April, as the last curbside piles of dirty gray snow grew smaller, Wes discovered a new source of income in Alan Schwartz's poker games. The Texas Hold'em game in Alan's basement had become a regular Saturday afternoon event. Wes had been avoiding

the game because in the past he'd nearly always lost, but he'd gotten talked into playing one day and, grudgingly, had bought in for
twenty dollars.

Determined to retain as much of his money as possible, he'd
played his cards conservatively. No bluffing, no long-shot draws,
no raises with anything less than top pair, folding with anything
less. His cautious play had paid off. He'd begun to win, slowly
and steadily. By the time the game broke up, he had doubled his
money.

After that, he played every Saturday. When Alan Schwartz
accused him of playing like an old lady, Wes just smiled and stacked
his chips. When Robbie told him he was freakishly lucky, Wes
shrugged and said he was due. Within a few weeks he had amassed
more than two hundred dollars in poker winnings.

One rainy Saturday in late April, he hit a lucky streak and
was up nearly eighty dollars. Robbie, watching sourly as Wes
raked in another pot, said, "You had trip kings. How come you
didn't raise?"

"You were doing the raising for me," Wes said.

"What a wuss. Poker is supposed to be about *betting*!"

Wes shrugged. "I thought you might have a flush."

"Tightass." Robbie pushed his chair back. "I'm out of here."
He threw on his jacket and stomped up the stairs.

Wes smiled. Turning a profit made it easy to put up with the
ribbing.

That day he walked home in the rain and thought about how
just three months ago he had been walking in the snow with June.
Funny how the longer he went without seeing her, the more dream-
like and unreal she became.

June had decided a week earlier to turn her cell phone off during the day. Because she was driving herself crazy checking it all the time, not to mention burning up minutes and hours talking to Wes. Not that she didn't love talking to him, but it had gotten to the point of obsession. So she left it off between eight in the morning and seven at night.

It was *hard*. By six o'clock every night, she was bursting with things to say that she couldn't say to anyone else. Sometimes it was so intense she could almost taste him.

Such a waste. You'll probably never see him again, said Sarcastic June. *Dad will get a job in Alaska. You'll be living in an igloo and eating seal blubber.*

"Shut up!" June muttered. She leaned forward over her dressing table and shook her head so her hair fell in front of her face. She stared through the tangled strands.

Time to grow up, said Pragmatic June.

"Grow up, yourself," June said. She flipped her hair back, ran her fingers through it, then went to work on her face. She was having a good week, complexion-wise, so there wasn't much to do. A little eyeliner, lipstick not much different from the natural color of her lips, a touch of eyebrow pencil. "Good enough for the Drood," she told herself.

The Drood was a notorious bar and dance club normally open to adults only, but on the first Saturday of every month they had an all-ages show from six until ten, with two bands. June had never been there, but she was going that night with the Three Ts.

At first, she had said no, but Tabitha had been relentless.

"It's totally cool," Tabitha had said. "Just like a real dance club, only they just serve soda and fruit drinks."

"They have piña coladas and Bloody Marys," Tara had added. "But with no alcohol. They kick everybody out at ten and open it up to adults. One time, Sheila Murphy hid in the bathroom and got to stay past ten. This guy bought her a Champagne Blue."

"What's a Champagne Blue?" June had asked.

"It has real champagne in it, and it's blue. She said it was really good."

"We should totally do that," Trish had said. "I want a Champagne Blue. I want two!"

"Wrathskell is playing. They're crazy."

"Rumfuddle too."

June had never heard of either band.

"*Everybody's* going to be there, June. You *have* to come."

In the end, she had agreed to go. But she wasn't going to hide out in any restrooms. Or drink any blue champagne. In fact, she was determined to have no fun whatsoever.

From: Wes
r u there?
Apr 23 21:16

"How come you aren't talking to June?"

Paula stood in the doorway to his bedroom, looking in at him. For weeks she had been observing him with catlike intensity, following his long-distance romance as if it was her own personal soap opera.

Wes, sprawled on his bed, lowered the X-Men comic he'd been reading. "I don't talk to her twenty-four hours a day."

"You should."

"Well, I don't. Besides, I already used all my minutes." He went back to reading the comic book. Because he was saving money for The Plan, he hadn't been buying any new comics lately, so he was rereading the last twelve issues of Astonishing X-Men.

"Are you going to go see her?" Paula asked.

"None of your business."

"I bet you are. You should take her to Paris, like in that movie."

"What movie?"

"The one where they go to Paris."

"You don't even know where Paris is," said Wes.

"In France."

"You don't know where France is."

"In Europe."

"Okay, you win. Now leave me alone."

Paula did not move. Wes concentrated on pretending she wasn't there. He had almost succeeded when she spoke again.

"She could come here. She could stay in my room."

Wes said nothing. After a time, Paula left. Wes put down the comic and closed his eyes and thought about Paula's first question: *How come you aren't talking to June?*

He did not have an answer. June had told him she was going phoneless during the day. He respected that. He even understood it. And she was right, talking and texting only at night made it better. But where was she tonight? Wes attempted to form a psychic link with her. He squeezed his eyes tight shut and stared at the spots and lines and patterns until a face emerged, fuzzy and indistinct. He made it into a June-shaped face, then added details.

He and June had spent hours back in March trying to send each other ESP messages. It never worked.

He didn't believe in ESP anyway.

Why hadn't she called him — or at least texted?

There could be lots of reasons. But the more time that passed, the more out of control the whole thing felt — he had no idea what was really going on with her in Omaha, what she was really thinking, what she might be doing on a Saturday night instead of calling.

"Are you asleep?"

Wes opened his eyes to find Paula standing over him in her pajamas, staring into his face with those enormous brown eyes.

"I thought you went away," he said.

"I came back. Are you sad?"

"No."

"You look sad."

"Isn't it time for you to go to bed?"

His cell phone chimed. A new text message.

"That's her," said Paula. She turned and shuffled off in her bunny slippers as Wes reached for the phone.

From: JKE

I am hiding in a bathroom stall.

Apr 23 21:57

CHAPTER
THIRTY-FOUR

THE DROOD, located in one of Omaha's grittier neighborhoods, looked like a dump from the outside — walls covered with graffiti, cigarette butts littering the sidewalk, double doors painted with several layers of black paint and studded with staples and the torn corners of old handbills . . . not the elegant nightclub she had imagined.

Inside, it was nicer. An old-fashioned mirrored disco ball hung above the dance floor, and a curved staircase led up to a balcony with lots of tables and chairs. There were two bars, one against the back wall and one upstairs. Several hundred noisy, energetic teens were milling about, waiting for the first band to start.

June followed Tabitha to the bar and ordered a Coke. The bartender put a slice of lime on the rim and set the drink on a coaster shaped like a guitar. She liked that. He charged her three dollars for it. That, she didn't like so much.

Tara and Trish were already on the dance floor, gyrating to the thumping house music while the first band — Rumfuddle or Wrathskell, she wasn't sure — set up their equipment on the stage.

Tabitha yelled something in June's ear.

"What?"

Tabitha pointed, grabbed June's arm, and pulled her across the room to a table where some kids she recognized from school were sitting. June and Tabitha dragged a couple of chairs up and joined them.

Bart Hanson, a quiet type in school, must have had a few beers before coming. He was talking — yelling, more like — something about a slasher movie he'd seen. Jenna Stiles must have been drinking too — she looked a little slack-faced and out of it. June didn't know the other two, who were trying to talk over Bart, relating their own favorite parts of the movie. Tabitha said something about slasher movies being stupid, and everybody started arguing loudly, but in a fun sort of way. June listened, trying to find a place to insert herself into the conversation, but she hadn't seen any slasher movies lately. After a few minutes, she got up and went to search for a restroom.

By the time she returned, the band had started playing. The table she had been sitting at was empty. She looked around, hoping to spot a familiar face. A tall guy wearing a black leather jacket and shredded jeans approached her from the bar, smiling.

"June?"

She stared at him.

"It's Kel," he said. "We met at school?"

"Oh!"

"You here by yourself?"

"No, I came with, uh, you know, Trish and Tara and Tabitha?"

"Tabitha Kane? I know Tabitha. You want something to drink?"

She didn't. But she said yes.

Over the next half hour, June learned a great deal about Kel Smith. He was a senior, he was Hills High's official audio geek, he drove a twenty-year-old Audi, he had a tattoo of a panther on his lower back, or so he claimed, and he liked about twenty bands she'd never heard of. He never asked anything about her — it was all about Kel, and Kel's plans. Typical guy. He said he planned to spend a year traveling after he graduated, then go to film school at USC to be a director. His best friend was playing bass guitar with Rumfuddle, the next band up.

"You'll like 'em," he said. "They're way better than these guys."

"Wrathkill?"

"Wrath*skell*. Rumfuddle's better. You want to dance?"

"Sure."

Kel's idea of dancing involved a lot of elbows flying and fists pumping, and he had one move that looked like he was trying to shake a tarantula out of his pant leg. Still, he was about a thousand times cooler than anybody she had ever expected to meet in Omaha, Nebraska.

As the dance floor got rowdier and more crowded, June and Kel became separated. June made it to the periphery without getting stepped on or elbowed. She spotted the Three Ts at a table up on the balcony level. She climbed up the spiral staircase and joined them.

"Was that Kel Smith you were with?" Trish asked.

June nodded, wondering what they would think of that.

"He's cool," Trish said.

"Kind of dangerous to dance with, though," June said.

Tabitha announced their plans to stay for the over-twenty-one show.

"You're going to hide in the restroom?" June said.

"Better," said Tabitha. "A couple of the Rumfuddle guys said they could get us into the band room."

"Where's that?"

"Behind the stage, down in the basement. We can wait there until after ten. Then come out and drink Champagne Blue. You in?"

"I don't know . . . I told my parents I'd be home by eleven."

"How will you get home?" Tabitha asked. They had come in her car.

June shrugged. "Maybe Kel can give me a ride."

After Wrathskell's set was over, she found Kel at the downstairs bar talking to some guys she didn't know.

"Thought I'd lost you," he said. "What's up?"

They talked for a few minutes, Kel telling her about people and bands she didn't know, and about a cool secondhand clothing store down by the Old Market. Rumfuddle replaced Wrathskell on the stage and launched a thumping, hypnotic beat, all drums and bass. Kel wanted to dance, but June told him she had a blister. He seemed to believe her.

"My friends are staying after hours," June said. "I was wondering if you could give me a ride home later? After the set?"

"Sure, no problem." He seemed distracted, looking out across the club. "Hey, there's Tony." He walked off. June wasn't sure if she was supposed to follow him or not, so she stayed put. After a few minutes of standing all by herself, she went back upstairs. The Ts were gone.

She did not love Rumfuddle's music. The beat was cool, but the lead singer had a whiny, high-pitched voice, and all of their songs were about misery and death. Kel had disappeared completely.

As ten o'clock approached, June began to get worried. She moved through the club, looking for a familiar face. There were a few kids she recognized from school, but she didn't know them well enough to beg a ride.

At five minutes to ten, the lights came up, Rumfuddle ended their set, and the underage crowd migrated toward the exit. June searched the crowd frantically. The Ts were nowhere in sight, and neither was Kel. She considered heading outside, trusting to luck to find a ride. She thought of herself standing pathetically alone on the littered sidewalk in that crappy neighborhood.

With the club ninety percent empty, June headed for the restroom.

CHAPTER
THIRTY-FIVE

From: Wes

Hiding in the bathroom? Why?

Apr 23 21:59

From: JKE

So the 3Ts cn have blue champagne. L8r

Apr 23 22:00

June had told Wes about the Three Ts, but he had no idea what "blue champagne" might be. A drink? A fabric color? A band? No idea. He laid back on his bed with his fingers laced behind his head, closed his eyes, and took The Plan through myriad variations: commercial airliner, hot air balloon, hitchhiking, hop a train, ride his bike, teleport. . . . He ran through dozens of scenarios of what would happen once he got there, and soon was caught up again in trying to construct a perfect image of June's face. . . .

The bedroom light flashed off and on. Wes opened his eyes and realized he had fallen asleep. His mother, wearing her terry cloth robe, was looking in at him.

"Are you going to sleep in your clothes?" she asked.

He sat up and shook his head.

"Good night, then," his mom said. She closed his door.

Wes changed into the gym shorts and T-shirt that served him for pajamas, brushed his teeth, and returned to bed. He sent a quick text to June, set his cell to vibrate, and balanced it on his chest so it would wake him if he fell asleep. He turned out the bedside lamp, closed his eyes, and waited.

At two minutes after ten, the restroom door opened. A man's voice called out, "Anybody in here?"

June, in the last stall, pulled her feet up so they couldn't be seen under the stall door. She held her breath, felt her pounding heart. The man went down the row of stalls, banging the doors open. He reached the last stall and banged his hand against the door.

"C'mon out, honey. Party's over."

June put her feet down and opened the stall door. A beefy, balding man wearing a polo shirt with DROOD written on the right side of the chest and MANNY on the left was standing there scowling at her.

"Every month, the same thing," he said. "You kids must think we're a bunch of idiots."

"Sorry," said June. Her face felt hot with embarrassment.

The man grabbed her arm, marched her out of the restroom, across the club, and out the door.

"Don't come back next month," he said. "I've had it." He went back inside.

June was not alone on the sidewalk. A dozen or so other underage kids were standing there looking at her with varied expressions: scorn, pity, amusement, disdain — just like all the Junes in her head. One guy had something sticking out the side of one nostril. It looked like the wishbone from a turkey.

June said, "Uh, anybody going up by Hills?"

Nobody was. June walked a few yards down the sidewalk and leaned against the cinder block wall, considering her options. She could take a cab, but she'd have to ask her parents for money when she got home, and that would mean a lecture, and they would never let her go out with the Ts again. She could walk, but that would take hours, and her shoes were already killing her. She could just wait for the Ts to come out, but they'd probably be drunk on blue champagne. Some of the people hanging outside the club looked iffy, especially the guy with the bone through his nose.

She took out her cell and was calling for a cab when she heard Tabitha's voice.

"Like we'd ever *want* to come back to your lame club!" Tabitha, Tara, and Trish were facing the bouncer, Manny.

"My ID says I'm twenty-one." Trish waved her fake license in his face.

"I don't care what it says, shorty," said Manny. "You're out of here."

The Three Ts set off haughtily down the sidewalk. June yelled, "Hey!"

Tabitha turned back and said, "Oh my God, June! We were so *worried* about you."

"Yeah, right," said June.

"That guy was a total jerk," Tara said.

"I guess it's his job," June said.

"He didn't have to be so mean about it," said Tabitha. "Creep. He touched my boob when he grabbed me. I should report him."

"What about Kel?" June asked.

"Him?" Tabitha sneered. "He left at ten."

SOMEONE WAS FIRING A VIBRATOR RAY into his sternum. Wes clutched at his chest and opened his eyes. It was dark. He was in bed, holding a vibrating, glowing cell phone.

"Hello?" His voice came out muddy with sleep.

"I'm mad at you."

"June?" He sat up, fumbling for the light.

"Who else?"

"Wait . . . what?" He could hear her breathing. "Are you okay?"

"No thanks to you!"

"I don't . . . start over. What?" He needed time to wake up. "Where are you?"

"In freaking *Omaha*! Where do you *think*?"

Wes cleared his throat. "Uh, what's going on?" He looked at his clock: 12:04.

"What do you care? You're in stupid Minnesota."

Stupid Minnesota? Wes tried to come up with something to say, but not quickly enough.

"I don't know why I bothered to call," June said. "You're obviously, like, half asleep."

"I'm not asleep."

"Good for you."

Wes's grogginess was turning to irritation.

"Look," he said, some edge to his voice, "why don't you just tell me what's going on."

"I was at this club," she said. "The Drood?"

Like he was supposed to know what she was talking about.

"Yeah?"

"I was with this guy."

"What guy?" he said quickly.

"It doesn't matter. Just a guy. His name is Kel."

Wes's heart started doing this thrum-thrum-thrum thing. His stomach felt as if it was melting and flowing into his bowels. He tried to speak, but nothing came out.

June said, "We were dancing, and he was supposed to give me a ride home, but he just took off and left me there, and you weren't anywhere, and stupid Tabitha and them were trying to drink blue champagne and this guy grabbed me in the bathroom and dragged me outside and just left me and it just really, really sucked. I could've got robbed or raped or something and you're all the way in stupid Minnesota and . . . and I *hate* you."

Her words were claws; Wes felt as if he'd been shredded. Part of him was listening, hearing her words, interpreting them, filing them in his memory, while another part wanted to throw himself through the phone line, to pop out of her cell like a genie from a bottle and hold her tight until everything was okay again. Still another piece of him wanted to slap her, to make her stop. And, from deep in the most ancient part of his brain came a powerful desire to beat this guy Kel to death with the thigh bone of an antelope.

And then there was the part of him that was in charge of his mouth.

"Why were you dancing with that guy?" he asked.

It took her a few seconds to reply.

"Because he was there," she said. "And you weren't."

June knew she was being completely unreasonable and illogical and ridiculous. She knew she would regret everything she said, and that she was hurting Wes with her words as surely as if she were stabbing him with a knife. She *wanted* to hurt him, to make him feel what she was feeling. Why else would she have mentioned Kel? Why else yell at Wes for something he had nothing to do with?

Wes wasn't saying anything.

"Are you there?" She heard the scrape of the phone against his cheek, then the softest of clicks, a hollow sound that was not a sound, and she was alone.

From one surviving corner of his mind — a tiny citadel that had managed to withstand the onslaught — Wes observed himself lying rigid on his bed in the dark and wondered if he would ever move again. He knew what was happening, but he could not make it stop. Anger, pain, and helplessness combined to paralytic effect.

The body will survive, he told himself. *I will be okay.*

Or maybe not. He focused on one body part: the index finger of his right hand, and tried to move it. The finger twitched. He made an effort to expand his rib cage, to draw air into his lungs, with only partial success.

What had just *happened*? He couldn't think about it, but he couldn't think about anything else, either. The thought of June with some guy, dancing, was unbearable, but he kept going back to that image, touching it to feel the pain.

Sleep? He would never sleep again.

After a time, he was able to turn his head to the side. The clock read 12:23. Less than twenty minutes had passed since June's call, yet it felt like hours. Daylight was still six hours away. How was he supposed to get through this night? Did he even *want* to make it to dawn? Spontaneous Human Combustion — that was the answer. He willed himself to burst into flames. He felt a spot of warmth in the vicinity of his liver, but it didn't last. That was the problem with SHC. It never happened when you needed it most. He forced the coherent part of his brain to think about other things. School. Eating apples. The garage floor, all stained and gritty from winter. Now that it was spring, his mom could park her car outside again. His breathing slowed and became deeper. He had to do something, *now*.

Something completely insane.

June had cried a normal amount when she was a kid. Cried because she skinned her knee, cried because of a sandbox fight with another child, cried because her tummy hurt, cried because she didn't get her way — the list of reasons to cry was long.

She no longer cried about those things. One day when she was twelve she had burned her hand while making French toast. That had hurt as much as anything had ever hurt her, but instead of crying she simply bit her lip and ran cold water over it until the pain became bearable, thinking, at the time, *I didn't cry!* It made her feel grown up and brave, and after that she cried less often, and when she did cry it was about different things — often things that made no sense. Like watching a really stupid movie. Or reading something in a book. Or sometimes it was about nothing at all, just a vast empty feeling that could only be soothed by a solitary bout of tears and snuffling.

That was different too. A little kid crying demanded an audience. Grown-up crying was best done alone.

Why was she crying now? Was it the empty feeling? No, it was more a feeling of helplessness, powerlessness, knowing what she wanted and needed but having no way to get it.

She wanted Wes. And she couldn't have him.

It was that simple.

12:42

12:43

12:44

THIRTY-SEVEN

From: JKE

Pls don't hate me.

Apr 24 00:46

Wes opened the garage door as slowly and quietly as he could, so as not to waken his parents. He put his mom's Toyota in neutral and positioned himself between the front of the car and the workbench at the back of the garage. He put his back against the bench and his feet on the car bumper and pushed. The car slowly moved toward the open door. He pushed harder. The back tires rolled over the lip of the garage onto the sloped driveway. Wes fell to the floor. He jumped up and ran after the car as it picked up speed, yanked open the driver's side door, jumped in, and hit the brake, stopping the car just before it rolled onto the street. He put the car in park and walked back into the garage.

Two hours later, Wes heard a sound and looked up to see his father standing in the open garage door wearing powder blue pajamas and his Sorels, holding a baseball bat in both hands.

"Wes, what the hell?" his dad said.

Wes said, "I couldn't sleep." He dunked the mop in the bucket of soapy water and wrung it out.

"You're cleaning the garage at three o'clock in the morning?"

"I'm almost done." Wes looked around the garage, at the clean floor, the orderly tool bench, the neatly arranged shelves. "It was supposed to be a surprise."

"You scared me half to death! I thought we were being robbed!"

"Sorry."

His mother's voice came from the house. "Frank? Is everything all right?"

"We're fine," Wes's dad said, raising his voice slightly. "It's your obsessive-compulsive neat-freak son!"

A few seconds later, Wes's mom came shuffling out to the garage in her bathrobe and slippers. "What on earth? Wes? What happened here?"

Wes sighed. "I just couldn't stand it," he said.

The three A.M. garage incident was not mentioned the next day, although his mom kept giving him worried looks. That afternoon, Wes went downstairs to the laundry room and folded all the clean clothes and linens that had been piling up in the hamper next to the dryer. His mom came down to see what he was doing.

"I'm trying to help out more," he told her.

"That's nice," she said, giving him another worried look.

Wes finished folding, then went to his room and called Alan Hurd.

"I need to talk to you," he said. "Can I come over?"

"Bring food," Alan said.

Alan Hurd shoved a handful of chips into his mouth and chewed, slowly and deliberately. Wes waited, knowing that to rush Alan at that point would only make him say no.

Alan swallowed, never taking his eyes off Wes.

"No," he said, reaching back into the bag for another handful of chips.

"Why not?"

"Because my parents won't let me drive it till school's out." Spitting potato chip fragments.

"Look, it's just sitting out behind your garage. It's not good to let a car sit for that long."

"My dad would kill me."

"He won't even notice it's gone. You can't see it from the house."

"It's not insured."

"I'll be careful." Wes could see he wasn't getting anywhere. "And I'll owe you forever. This is really important to me. Seriously."

"I didn't even know you were still talking to her," Alan said.

"I didn't want to tell anybody."

"Not even me?" Alan said, looking peeved.

"Not even anybody. I just — I didn't want you guys to think I was pathetic."

"You *are* pathetic. Secret long-distance girlfriend? That's as bad as Schwartz and his used *Penthouse*."

"It would just be for a couple days."

Alan sat back in his seat, refilled his mouth with chips, washed them down with a glug of orange soda, belched loudly.

"No," he said. He was enjoying this. The begging.

"I'll bring it back with a full tank. I'll pay you. I'll, like, rent it."

Alan considered.

"How much?" he said.

Wes called June that night and they talked, but neither of them brought up June's midnight phone call from the night before. They talked about music, people, TV shows, whether it would be better to live on a tropical island or on top of a mountain, Nebraska hamburgers versus Minnesota burgers — they never had trouble finding things to talk about. But they didn't talk about the Drood, or Kel, or how Wes had hung up on her. It was there, a dark scary cloud, but neither of them wanted to bring it up.

Monday after school, Wes washed his mom's car. After dinner, he called the other Alan, Alan Schwartz, and asked him to host a forty-eight-hour poker game the coming weekend.

"I don't think so," said Alan. "My mom barely tolerates the Saturday afternoon game."

"She won't have to know," Wes said.

"Oh, she'd know. My mom's practically telepathic, especially with six or seven of us in her basement."

"It'll be an *imaginary* game," Wes said.

Alan said, "Explain."

Later, just before dinner, Wes mentioned the big game to his mom.

She said, "Forty-eight *hours*? Good Lord, Wes! Mrs. Schwartz is okay with that?"

"Sure. We never leave the basement. It's self-contained. She'll hardly know we're there."

"Seven teenage boys in her basement? She'll know you're there, all right."

"She likes it. She says she'd just as soon know where her son is all weekend."

"What about sleeping? How will you sleep?"

"No sleep," Wes said. "That's the idea. It's like an endurance contest."

"How much money do you boys play for, anyway?"

"Just nickels and dimes," Wes said. He was surprised by how easily the lies came out of his mouth. "I'll be a couple miles away. And you can call me on my cell anytime."

She frowned, not liking it. "When will you be home?"

"Forty-eight hours, like I said. Four o'clock Friday to four o'clock Sunday."

Her frown eased somewhat. "Let me talk to your father when he gets home from work."

The next morning, before leaving for school, Wes washed the breakfast dishes. His mother, sipping her coffee, watched him suspiciously.

"Wes, you are scaring me," she said.

"Why?"

"That's what I'd like to know."

It was simple. He was building up points. Because there was a good chance that something would go wrong, that his parents would find out what he was doing, that everything would go wrong. So for the next few days, he would be the best, most responsible son anyone could possibly want.

Just in case.

THIRTY-EIGHT

THEY WERE TALKING ON THE PHONE — never mind that it was costing her twenty-five cents a minute — and June was telling Wes about Trish getting in trouble, when she heard beeping.

"What's that?" she asked.

"Um . . . I'm playing this game?"

"You're playing a computer game while I'm talking to you?"

"I'm listening!" Wes said. "You were telling me about Trish, uh, writing something on the school wall —"

"She wrote it on Tabitha's *locker*!"

"That's what I meant."

"And she got caught."

"Oh yeah?" *Beep.*

She hung up.

He called back five seconds later.

"Sorry," he said when she picked up. "I turned it off."

"I should feel honored?"

"June . . ."

"At least you got my name right."

"I wanted to talk to you about something."

"Okay, sure. Hang on a sec while I boot up *World of Warcraft*." She didn't actually have *World of Warcraft*, but it was the only game she could think of.

"Yeah, right," he said.

She disconnected.

What was happening? Why was she so mad at him all the time? And why was he playing a computer game instead of listening to her?

Her phone went *bee-boop*, the incoming text message sound. She glared at the phone, then picked it up.

From: Wes

What r u up to Friday nite?

Apr 27 6:29

June puzzled over the message. What was she *up to* Friday night? Why would he care? It was none of his business. Or maybe he was thinking about her and just asking, in a good way, not in a suspicious, nosy way. Was he jealous? If there was one thing she couldn't stand it was jealousy. She'd had a jealous boyfriend once. It was creepy.

What was *happening*?

Whatever it was, it wasn't good.

The next morning, June woke up, brushed her teeth, and was halfway dressed before she even thought about Wes. When she did, it was as if a six-hundred-pound *thing* had settled onto her shoulders. She let out a little squeak, not quite a scream, then clapped a hand over her mouth.

"Junie? Are you all right?"

"I'm *fine*," she yelled down the stairs to her mom. "It's *nothing!*"

She finished dressing, then checked her cell for new messages. There weren't any. She turned off the phone and put it in her top dresser drawer and went down to the kitchen, where her mom was making oatmeal, part of her new healthy eating routine. June poured herself half a cup of coffee, filled it to the top with milk, added a spoonful of honey, and gave it thirty seconds in the microwave.

"Usually when people scream," her mother said, "it's *some*thing."

"I thought I saw a mouse," June said.

"In your bedroom?"

"It was a crazed dust bunny."

"Time to sweep under your bed."

June shrugged.

"How's Wes?"

June did not reply.

"Since you seem determined to stay in contact with the boy, I should at least get the occasional progress report."

"He plays computer games while we're talking."

Her mom laughed and put a bowl of oatmeal in front of her. June doctored it with a thick slab of butter and a heaping table-spoon of sugar.

Her mother said, "Sort of defeats the healthy lifestyle initiative."

"*Your* initiative," June said. "I have no lifestyle."

THIRTY-NINE

The Drood
wuz rood.

"Thursdays suck," said Tara.

"Wednesdays suck worse," said Trish. She pushed her half-eaten taco aside. "I was here until almost five yesterday cleaning lockers."

"You're right," Tabitha said. "Yesterday was Wednesday."

"And besides, it's not like I defaced fifty lockers. I just wrote on yours."

"It's nice and clean now," Tabitha said. "Thank you."

"I think it should be illegal to force students to be janitors."

"What did you write, anyway?" Tara asked.

"Nothing. It was stupid."

"Something horrible and filthy," Tabitha said.

Trish flicked a shred of lettuce at Tabitha.

"Hey!"

"It was a poem about the rude Drood," Trish said.

"Why didn't you write it on *your* locker?"

"I was sharing."

June, who had said nothing all through lunch, followed the conversation the way she might watch a movie in Chinese with no subtitles. It was just about batting sounds back and forth, passing the time, getting somebody to look at you, to acknowledge your existence. The meanings of the words didn't matter. If she said something, would any of them actually hear her?

She said, quietly, "I think I might be breaking up with my boyfriend."

The three Ts looked at her uncomprehendingly for a second, then Tara said, "I hate Mondays most."

"Every day sucks except Saturday," said Trish. She forced open the remains of her taco with a fork and picked at the shreds of white cheese.

June said, "He plays on his computer while we're talking."

"We should do a poll," Tabitha said. "Vote on which day of the week is the suckiest."

When June didn't reply to either of his last two texts, Wes felt his resolve harden. He wouldn't call her, or let her know in any way that he was coming. Because what if he did, and she told him not to come? The best thing would be to simply show up.

Friday after school, he stuffed a change of clothes into his backpack and set off for Alan Hurd's. When he arrived, Mrs. Hurd told him Alan wasn't home.

"He said for you to meet him at Alan Schwartz's," she said.

Wes walked the eight blocks to Alan Schwartz's. He was surprised to find Robbie and Calvin there, as well as Alan Hurd. They were in the basement setting up the card table.

"I decided your idea wasn't so unfeasible after all," Alan Schwartz said.

"Which idea?" Wes asked.

"The forty-eight-hour poker marathon. Why not do it? Worst-case scenario, my mother has a paroxysm and kicks everybody out. It wouldn't be the first time. You sure you don't want to play?"

"I just want my parents to *think* I'm playing."

Alan Hurd handed him a set of car keys. "I started it up last night," he said. "It runs fine, but keep an eye on the oil. And don't crash it."

Alone, heading south on I-35, speedometer steady at seventy miles per hour, a road map and a four-pack of Red Bull for company, Wes felt free. He cranked up the volume on a mix CD he'd burned for June and tried not to think about what he would do when he got there.

What he would say.

What she would say.

FORTY

WES HAD BEEN THINKING OF OMAHA as a small town plunked down in the middle of a wheat field that covered the entire state of Nebraska. It wasn't like that at all. Omaha was huge, hilly, and horrendously complicated. He arrived at the city limits at ten fifteen; it was after eleven by the time he found June's house. He sat in his car looking at it — a large, two-story, brick-front house with a horseshoe driveway — hardly believing that he was really there, that only seven hours ago he had been in Minnesota, that June was behind those walls.

Only one light on. One of the upstairs rooms. He got out of the car and called her on his cell.

The phone rang four times, then went to voice mail. Wes hung up, redialed, and sent her a text. He waited. Thirty seconds later, the curtains parted, and he saw her face.

June pulled back from the window.

She looked in the mirror, winced, forced herself to breathe. She threw on a pair of jeans and a hoodie, checked herself in the mirror again, ran a brush through her hair, and checked her breath. She went to the window. He was still there, leaning against a car, illuminated by yellow light from the streetlamp. Wes had a car? What else hadn't he told her?

She left her room as quietly as possible, creeping past her parents' bedroom with her sneakers in her hand. At the front door, she silenced the alarm system and let herself out.

He was still there. She sat on the front step and pulled on her sneakers. He just stood there by his car. Why wasn't he walking toward her? She stood up and started toward him, and he began moving toward her. June could hear herself breathing, and as they grew closer, she could hear him breathing too. They both stopped with three feet between them. She was breathing hard.

He reached out his hand.

June stepped back.

Wes heard himself make a sound, a sudden inhalation. His hand fell to his side, dead weight.

"Just wait," June said.

He waited. He couldn't have moved if he'd wanted to.

"I want to see you," she said, her eyes scanning his face.

Wes stared back at her, trying to take it in. She looked different. It wasn't just the shorter hair, or the eyes. He couldn't tell if she had on her colored contacts; her irises looked more gray than blue in the glow of the streetlamp. What felt different, he decided, was the nearly unbearable tension in her body.

She moved, one small step, and then another, and then they were standing mere inches apart, their breath mingling in the cool late night air. She raised her hand and touched her fingers to his lips. There was a missing moment, as if time had stuttered, then they had their arms around each other, their mouths pressed hard together, the street, the city, the planet, the universe spinning around them. And then they broke apart, both of them gasping.

June said, "Oh, crap."

Wes knew exactly what she meant. He laughed. The laugh came out high-pitched, then broke, and she started laughing too. They came together again, this time a gentle, almost fragile embrace. June sighed, her body softening and molding itself against his chest.

She whispered, "What are we going to do?"

Wes cleared his throat and said, "You want to get something to eat?"

They found a truck stop on I-80, just outside of town. June had never been in a real truck stop before — her parents, when traveling, always stopped at chain restaurants because, in her mother's words, "You can trust the food."

"Yeah, trust the food to be bad," June had said.

The food at the truck stop was pretty good, judging from the way Wes tore through his Hungry Driver — an enormous breakfast of fried eggs, pancakes, sausage, bacon, hash browns, and toast.

"I think the twenty-four-hour breakfast should be law," he said, biting into his third sausage link. "How are your fries?"

"A little soggy," June said.

Most of the other customers were real truckers — men wearing baseball caps, a lot of them with beards, rough-looking but not scary rough. Most of the tables and booths were empty. Only one waitress was working, a forty-something woman with big blond hair, a floral tattoo peeking up from her ample bosom, and a name tag that read PHLOX.

"I always thought you had to be a trucker to eat at one of these places," June said as Phlox topped off their coffees.

"We don't care what you drive, honey," Phlox said with a heavily mascaraed wink. "Long as you eat and pay."

So far, she and Wes hadn't talked about anything important.

"So who's this guy Kel?" Wes finally blurted out.

It took June a few seconds to respond. "Just this guy," she said. She told him the story of what had happened at the Drood. "I'm sorry I got mad at you."

"It's okay."

Wes told her how he'd paid Alan Hurd to borrow his car, and that Jerry and Naomi were going to prom together. "They've both calmed down now that the election is over," he said. He told her about playing poker, and his job at Jamba Juice. They sat there for almost two hours, drinking cup after cup of coffee and talking.

"I think we should move to France," June said.

Wes said, "Okay. Why France?"

"I want to try real French fries."

"We'll need money."

"We can rob a bank."

Wes grinned. "Bonnie and Clyde."

"I never saw that."

"Everybody dies in the end."

"Oh." June noticed their waitress looking at them from the counter. "I think Phlox is giving us the stink eye."

"What time is it?"

"After two."

"We should probably go."

"Go where?"

"I'm not going to sleep the whole weekend," Wes said.

They were driving aimlessly through the streets of Omaha. June was snuggled as close to him as she could get, the console digging into her side, her head resting on Wes's shoulder.

"I'm not sleepy either," she said. The one thing they hadn't talked about was what would happen next.

"I had a plan," Wes said. "I was going to buy Calvin's brother's bike, and as soon as school was out, I was going to drive down here and find a place to stay and get a job. But I couldn't wait."

June was flattered. More than flattered — it was the most romantic thing any guy had ever done for her. But now what?

"I have to go back Sunday morning," he said.

June said, "Oh."

"My parents think I'm at Schwartz's, playing a poker marathon. And I have to get the other Alan's car back."

"It must be really inconvenient having two Alans as friends."

"It's horrible. I should get rid of one."

"Which?"

"Flip a coin."

"What time is it?"

"Four fifty-seven."

"My mom gets up at six."

Neither of them said anything for a very long time.

"Turn left up here," June said.

Wes turned. He had been behind the wheel for so long the car felt like an extension of his body.

June said, "My parents would freak if they knew you were here."

"Why?"

"They just would. Turn right at the light."

Wes turned. He recognized the neighborhood. Curvy streets, big houses. He noticed a car behind him, but didn't think about it. He pulled up in front of June's house.

"It's only five thirty," he said. "We can sit here for a while."

The inside of the car became suddenly, shockingly, as bright as day. An electronic voice boomed, practically rattling the windows.

"Step out of the car!"

Wes looked back and was blinded by the light.

"Step out of the car and put your hands in the air!"

FORTY-ONE

WES REMEMBERED WHAT FOLLOWED like flashes of a nightmare:

Bent over the hood of his car, the cop's rough hands on his body, checking him for weapons. "It's not stolen!" Wes kept saying. "It's my friend's car!"

The policeman did not seem to hear him.

Mrs. Edberg in her bathrobe, opening the front door.

June's face looking at him from the backseat of the second squad car.

"I have to talk to her!" Wes said.

"Shut up, kid," said the cop.

Mr. Edberg, in pajamas and a raincoat, standing on his front lawn, talking to the police.

What was he telling them?

The long ride downtown, Wes telling the cops over and over that it was all a big mistake.

Sitting in the juvenile holding tank with one other guy, a drunk kid of maybe fourteen, his shirt stained with vomit, lying on his side on the concrete floor, curled into a ball, crying.

He's me, *Wes thought, staring at the miserable kid.* The way he is, that's the way I feel.

The phone call . . .

"Dad?"

"Wes? What the hell?" His father did not appreciate being awakened at six A.M. on a Saturday morning.

"Dad, I'm sorry."

"Where are you?" His voice changed from irritation to concern.

"I'm . . . uh . . . I'm in jail. But I didn't do it!"

"Calm down, Wes." His dad's voice moved into competent, businesslike mode. "Where are you, exactly?"

"Nebraska," said Wes.

Wes had never been so embarrassed in his life. His parents would never trust him again. The ride back to the Twin Cities lasted a lifetime.

For the first half hour, they had talked. Wes told them everything. What else could he do? He told them everything. His parents, in the front seat, listened without comment. Nothing they might do to him could possibly be worse than having to listen to himself. He sounded like the biggest moron on the planet.

After he had finished, nobody said anything for what must have been a hundred miles. They were approaching Des Moines when his dad cleared his throat and spoke.

"Wes. What are we going to do with you?"

"I don't know," Wes said.

He really didn't.

"What are we going to do with her?" June's mother said.

The three of them were sitting in the breakfast nook, Dad with his coffee, Mom drinking tea, June with her hands in her lap.

Her dad was wearing a suit even though it was Saturday. Her mom was still in her robe.

"For one thing," her father said, "she has to cease communications with that boy."

"His name is Wes," said June.

"She can't just turn her emotions on and off, El," said her mother.

"This is why we don't look back," her father said. "We move on."

"She's a teenager."

They were talking about her as if she wasn't there.

"She's a young woman," her father said. "A hundred years ago, she'd already be married with children. She's perfectly capable of making good decisions."

"I'm sitting right here," June said.

Her parents both looked at her.

Her mom said, "Honey, what were you thinking?"

"He drove all the way here," said June.

"In a stolen car!" her father said.

"It wasn't stolen. He borrowed it from his friend."

"So he says."

"He drove all the way from Minnesota to see me. We just went for a ride. Is that so bad?"

"You're seventeen," said her mother.

"Yeah, and like Dad says, a hundred years ago, I'd be considered an adult!"

"That was then. This is now."

"I'm sorry," said June. "I can't help it that I like him."

"Then it's time you learned to *un*like him," her father said. "Starting now."

June felt herself shrinking into a small, hard knot. There was no way. Wes was planted deep inside her, so deep that no amount of wishing or hoping or parental brainwashing could ever dislodge him. But trying to tell that to her father would be arguing with a stone. All she could do was go along with him, or at least pretend.

She said, "Okay."

Her father's expression softened. "I know it's hard, Junie. But these things . . . they pass. The things you're feeling, they're learned behaviors. Chemical signals. Your brain can develop new pathways; your mind is yours to control. It's no different from learning to not suck your thumb, or quitting smoking —"

"I don't smoke," June muttered.

"— or learning a new language, or any other form of personal improvement. You can . . ." He droned on. June had heard it all before, the Elton Edberg theory of maximizing personal development, what he called "biomechanical engineering." Any moment now, he would blurt out *"Next!"* and it would be all she could do to keep herself from dumping his coffee in his lap, which wouldn't help.

June looked desperately at her mother, who rolled her eyes, then stood up and accidentally on purpose jostled the table. Elton Edberg's coffee cup jumped and sloshed, spilling part of its contents onto the table. He jumped up, trying to avoid the river of coffee making its way across the tabletop. His thighs hit the edge of the table; the coffee cup tipped over completely and soaked the front of his pant leg. He cursed and swiped ineffectually at the wet spot with a napkin.

"Oh, great. I have a meeting at ten!" he said.

"You'd better change, then," said her mother.

As her father stalked off to his bedroom to put on a new suit, June looked gratefully at her mother.

Thank you, she mouthed.

"WHAT WAS I SUPPOSED TO DO?" Alan Hurd said. "My dad noticed that the car was gone. I don't know what he was doing back behind the garage. And all I said was that I didn't know what happened to the car. So he reported it stolen."

"You could have told him the truth," Wes said. It was Monday. They were standing outside the lunchroom in the hallway.

"You don't know my dad. Anyways, I just figured you'd drop the car off when you got back and everything would be fine. He'd never know. I sure didn't think you'd get pulled over in Omaha."

"Well, I did. And now my life is ruined."

"They dropped the charges. I don't see what the big deal is."

"The big deal is now I have to pay my parents back for the gas they used to drive down there, and I have to pay *your* dad to fly to Omaha and drive your stupid car back, which is, like, all the money I've saved my whole life, and my parents will never trust me again."

Alan shrugged. "I told you it was a bad idea in the first place."

Wes wanted to hit him, hard, right on the mouth. But he didn't, because he knew he might have done the same thing in Alan's place. Besides, if he got caught fighting in school again after the thing that had happened with Jerry, it would mean an automatic expulsion.

"Thanks a lot." Wes started to walk away.

Alan said, "Don't forget, you owe me a hundred bucks. For the rental."

Wes wheeled around, fists clenched.

Alan laughed nervously and backed away, saying, "Kidding! Kidding!"

Wes opened his hands and forced his fingers to relax, forced himself to breathe.

Alan said, "Are you going to play at Schwartz's Saturday?"

"Screw you," Wes said, and walked away.

The good thing — the *only* good thing — was that his parents hadn't taken away his cell phone. The bad thing — one of *many* bad things — was that June wasn't answering hers. Wes supposed that her parents had confiscated it, so he held off on the texting. But he kept trying to call, and by the end of the week he was having all these paranoid thoughts, like she still had her phone but didn't want to talk to him because he'd done such an incredibly stupid thing by driving to Omaha and getting thrown in jail and almost getting *her* thrown in jail too. And getting her in trouble with her parents, and who knew what all else. And he was actually thinking of stealing — for real this time — Alan's car, and driving back to Omaha. But not really. He didn't know what he was thinking. He couldn't stand it. Sitting in class. Seeing people looking at him — because thanks to Alan and his big mouth, everybody in school knew what had happened.

They took her cell phone and made her swear to not talk to Wes for a week.

"You need time to be in your own head," her father said.

"I *am* in my own head," June said, looking to her mom.

Her mother shrugged and looked away. June understood that to mean that while her mom sympathized with her, she was committed to maintaining a united parental front. So much for divide and conquer.

Her father put his hands on her shoulders and looked into her eyes. "One week, then we have another conversation."

June nodded.

Monday, at school, June told the Three Ts what had happened. At first it was gratifying to tell the story — her boyfriend stealing a car and driving all the way to Omaha was big-time romantic. Even if he hadn't really stolen the car. The Ts were goggle-eyed with admiration and astonishment.

"So is he in jail?" Tabitha asked.

"His parents came and got him. I think he's home now."

"Did you *talk* to him?"

June shook her head.

"Oh my God, you *absolutely* have to call him!" Trish said.

"I can't. I promised my parents I wouldn't talk to him for a week. Besides, they took my cell."

"Use mine!" Tabitha pulled out her cell.

"Are you kidding? You want to get me kicked out?"

Tabitha rolled her eyes and stuffed her phone back in her purse.

It was only six more days.

At home, June went through the motions, doing her homework, her laundry, helping with dinner, acting like a good little biomechanical daughter.

When she went to bed that night, June took inventory of her brain, an exercise of which her father would have approved. She imagined her mind as a big old house, like the one they'd lived in when she was a little girl: three stories plus an attic, huge walk-in closets, fancy wood trim everywhere. Her third-story bedroom was for her secret thoughts, the things she never talked about with anyone, the things that if she ever said them out loud might get her thrown into an institution. The hallways were for moving thoughts from room to room. The kitchen was for practical things, like how to tie a shoe, or remembering that two cups is the same as a pint. The master bedroom, where her parents slept, was for the things they told her, like how to behave and when to feel guilty. The big living room with the tall windows and the out-of-tune baby grand piano that none of them could play was where her thoughts swirled and collided. The cellar was for the things she feared: loneliness, toads, clowns, pain.

June walked herself through the house, moving from room to room, dodging uncomfortable thoughts, remembering things she hadn't thought about since forever. She opened the cellar door, then shut it quickly. She climbed back to the third floor, spent some time in her bedroom, then opened the door that led to the attic. She climbed the narrow staircase, brushing aside spiderwebs of thought. The attic was bright with sunlight blasting in through the large octagonal window at the west end. Nothing but a few boxed memories, abandoned dreams, and countless sparkling dust motes. She walked to the window and wiped the dust away with her sleeve. Outside was paradise, a beautiful green garden stretching as far as she could see.

June backed away from the window, then transported herself back to her bedroom with its strange, comforting, deeply personal thoughts.

Where was Wes? Not in the house, but someplace. She could feel his presence. She moved her awareness outside of her head — once again she was in her real bedroom, in Omaha.

If she opened her eyes, she would see the digital hour and minute projected onto the ceiling.

She kept her eyes closed.

She could feel her heart beating. She tried to imagine what it looked like. She knew that the human heart was a complicated muscle pumping red blood through arteries and veins. Still, it did not feel like a thing of flesh. It felt like the throbbing nucleus of her being, the fiery core of her galaxy. And her heart was not located in that three-story house. The house was in her head. Maybe her dad was right. The things in her head — those she could control. Doors would open and shut, blinds and curtains would close, rooms could be rearranged. But what was in her heart . . . was that forever?

SUMMER

FORTY-THREE

FOLLOW THE BLUE STRING, walk two paces, raise the heavy steel bar, jab it into the soil. Rock the bar back and forth to enlarge the hole, set the bar aside. Tease a seedling from the bundle riding on his back, bend over and place it into the hole, and gently pack the soil around its roots. Pick up the steel bar, follow the blue string two paces, repeat.

Each bundle contained five hundred seedlings. According to Chuckles Johanson, one man should be able to plant a bundle a day. Wes could manage about sixty seedlings per hour. At his current rate, planting five hundred trees would take eight hours, not counting time for breaks and lunch.

There were a hundred thousand seedlings to be planted. Wes, Robbie, and two other guys arrived at Johanson's Christmas Trees every morning at six. They were paid fourteen cents for every seedling planted, or seventy bucks a bundle.

A week ago, when Robbie had offered him the job on his uncle's tree farm, Wes had quit his Jamba Juice job and signed on. The money had sounded pretty good. But after ramming that steel bar into the hard ground for three hours, a knot of pain had formed between his shoulder blades, his palms were blistering, and his leg muscles felt like molten rubber.

Jab, rock, bend, plant.

So far, he had planted about forty dollars' worth of trees.

Jab, rock, bend, plant.

It was better than sitting around the house, doing nothing.

Jab, rock, bend, plant.

Every time he rammed the chiseled tip of the bar into the earth, a shock wave ran up his arms, smacked him in the back of his skull, and scrambled his thoughts.

Jab, rock, bend, plant.

Two thousand Christmas trees per acre. Fifty acres.

Jab, rock, bend, plant.

Were there Christmas tree farms in Nebraska?

Jab, rock, bend, plant.

June thought it was funny, him planting Christmas trees. "You're like Johnny Christmas Tree," she said.

Jab, rock, bend, plant.

It was only funny if you weren't the one who had to do it for ten hours a day.

Jab, rock, bend, plant.

His plan to spend the summer in Omaha had died. He had killed it by being stupid. So stupid.

Jab, rock, bend, plant.

Every dollar he had saved had gone to pay back his parents and Alan's father. His parents didn't trust him. June's parents thought he was a dangerous delinquent.

Jab, rock, bend, plant.

He and June were still talking on the phone, but without a future, it got harder and harder to find things to talk about.

Jab, rock, bend, plant.

He was sick of talking about France. Stupid, impossible fantasy. He didn't even like French fries that much.

Jab, rock, bend, plant.

Their phone conversations were getting shorter.

Jab, rock, bend, plant.

Some days, he couldn't remember her face.

Jab, rock, bend, plant.

Her face.

June was in her bedroom, reading one of her mom's romance novels, when she heard her parents talking.

Or rather, she *didn't* hear them.

Normally, her dad was a loud talker, and her mom was medium loud. If they were having a conversation downstairs, she could hear most of what they were saying, if she wanted to. Almost none of it was worth listening to, so she didn't pay much attention. But what she heard now was a low, almost subsonic murmur. Which meant that whatever they were saying, they didn't want her to hear it.

She put her book down and went to stand in the hallway at the top of the stairs. She could tell they were in the kitchen, but she still couldn't make out their words. Barefoot, she started slowly down the stairs. One of the middle steps was creaky; she couldn't remember which one.

Creak.

The low voices abruptly stopped. Busted. June walked quickly down the stairs and into the kitchen. Mom was sitting at the table. Dad was standing with his back to the sink. June could tell from their expressions that whatever they'd been talking about, it had to do with her.

"What's up?" she asked, making her voice all perky.

Her parents looked at each other, then back at her.

"What?" she said. June wasn't exactly scared, but she could feel herself tensing up inside, steeling herself to hear something she maybe wouldn't like. "Did Dad get fired again?"

"I did *not* get fired again!" he said, as if it was the most outrageous thing imaginable.

"Are we moving again?"

Her mom smiled. "Not exactly," she said.

At ten, Chuckles came riding over the hill in his ATV, parked at the edge of the field, and waved Wes over. Wes put down his bundle of seedlings and the steel bar and walked over to meet him. Robbie, who was working the other side of the field, did the same.

On the back of the ATV was a ten-gallon orange thermos filled with ice-cold lemonade. Wes and Robbie sucked down two paper cups each as Chuckles grinned and nodded.

It was easy to see how Chuckles had got his nickname. His lined, suntanned face remained fixed in a wide grin, even when he wasn't happy. Robbie had told Wes that his perpetual grin was the result of a piece of shrapnel from a Viet Cong mortar. The reconstructive surgery had left him with a permanent smile.

"You boys are doing a great job," Chuckles said.

Wes poured himself another cup of lemonade as Robbie sat down in the scant shade offered by the ATV.

"How're the backs holding up?" Chuckles asked.

"Kinda sore," Wes said.

Chuckles bobbed his head. "Couple days, you'll get used to it. You'll get strong!" He flexed his biceps.

Wes said, "Uh, Chuckles —" It felt weird to be calling the old man by such a silly name. "How come you don't have a . . . like, a planting machine to do this? Somebody must make one."

"Sure they do, but those babies cost money. Besides, hand-plants have a better chance of growing up straight and tall. Nobody wants a crooked Christmas tree. Also, if I had a machine, I couldn't be offering you young fellows work for the summer."

"He likes watching us slave in the hot sun," Robbie said.

Chuckles's grin widened. "That I do."

Instead of getting faster as the day wore on, Wes's planting speed decreased. Chuckles told him he could knock off at five, but Wes was determined to plant his entire bundle. By the time he finished, he was practically dead with fatigue.

Chuckles was impressed. "You did good, kid," he said, clapping Wes on the back. Wes nearly fell over.

Wes didn't get home until after eight. He would have walked straight to his room and flopped down on the bed, but his mom guessed what he had in mind and made him take a shower and eat a sandwich.

As he ate his sandwich, she chided him for not wearing sunscreen.

"Look at you, you're burnt to a crisp."

"I put some on," Wes said. "It must have sweated off."

"Use more next time," she said.

"Okay, whatever."

"Will you be working such long hours every day?"

"Hope not. It was my first day. Chuckles says we'll get faster."

"Well, I don't think he should be working you boys so hard."

"It's good for him." Wes's dad came into the kitchen for a glass of water. "Hard work never hurt anybody."

"Tell that to my back," Wes said.

"By the way," his mom said, "your cell phone has been ringing off the hook."

"My cell phone is on a hook?"

"You know what I mean. That incessant buzzing coming from your room every hour or so."

"Sorry. I meant to leave it off." Wes finished his sandwich quickly and ran upstairs to check his phone.

> From: JKE
> **OMG CALL ME CALL ME CALL ME CALL**
> **ME CALL ME CALL ME CALL ME CALL ME**
> **CALL ME!!!!!!**
> Jun 15 9:59

JUNE'S MOTHER HAD PREPARED A LIST — typed, single-spaced, two pages long.

"You're seventeen," she said by way of opening the discussion.

"So you keep telling me," June said.

Her mom gave her a sharp look.

"Sorry," said June, silently telling Sarcastic June to shut up.

"Yes, well, Dad and I have been talking, and we think that despite what happened last month — with Wes — we think we can trust you."

"You can," June said, wondering if it were true.

"All things considered, Wes seems like a nice boy. And you seem quite serious about him."

June nodded eagerly.

"Of course, your new job in Minneapolis will keep you busy most of the time, and I cannot express how important this job is."

June nodded somberly. Her job at the Minneapolis branch of Benford Bank, a temporary position, would be working with an army of other temps assembling the world's most intricate and difficult jigsaw puzzle. Several days earlier, someone at the bank had dumped six thousand deposited checks into the bank's paper shredder, along with several bags of other paper trash. The problem was that the checks had not yet been recorded or canceled, so now the bank had a Dumpster full of shredded paper. June's job would be to sort through those tiny strips of paper, separate the ones that had once been parts of checks, separate those by color and pattern, then puzzle the strips together to reconstruct each individual check.

"Why do people still use paper checks, anyway?" June asked. "Haven't they ever heard of check cards?"

Her mom laughed. "After this, I imagine the bankers are asking themselves the same question. They've asked Dad to spend six weeks — possibly longer — up in Minneapolis. They are showing a great deal of trust in El. This could lead to a permanent position."

"In Minneapolis?"

"Yes, possibly. Nothing is for sure, so I'll be staying on here — at least until we see how things go."

June pointed at the list on the table between them. "So what's that?"

"Rules."

"That's a lot of rules!"

"Do you want to go to Minneapolis or not?"

"Sorry," said June.

Her mother looked at the top sheet. "Rule number one. No sex."

"Mom!" June felt her face go red. "We are not having sex!"

"I'm not saying you did, or you would, or you wouldn't. I just want to be perfectly clear."

"That's pretty clear. Is kissing okay?"

"I trust your judgment in that regard. Number two. You will be home by ten o'clock every night, no exceptions."

"Then when are we supposed to have sex?" June asked.

Her mom gave her the raised-eyebrow look.

"Kidding!" said June.

"Rule number three. You will be responsible for keeping house for your father. That means cooking, cleaning, shopping, and laundry."

"All the time?"

"Dad will be working long hours, and he'll need you to take care of him."

"But I'll be working too!"

"June . . ."

"Okay, okay. Next?"

"Four. No drugs or drinking. At *all*."

"Gee, and here I was planning on developing a heroin habit," said Sarcastic June before June could stop her.

"Rule four-point-five. No sarcasm."

"You just made that up!" June said.

"Rule four-point-five-one. No arguing about the rules."

June bit her lip and nodded.

"Rule five. Keep your cell phone with you at all times. Rule six. Call me every day. Rule seven . . ."

There were thirty-six rules. June clamped her mouth firmly shut and listened numbly as her mother proceeded to restrict her future behavior in every way imaginable. She pushed aside Sarcastic June, Fearful June, Scornful June, and all the others, telling herself over and over that tomorrow she would be with Wes, and that was all that mattered.

FORTY-FIVE

HE WAS GETTING FASTER.

Jab, rock, bend, plant.

His movements had become robot efficient, as rhythmical as hip-hop — perfectly timed, flawlessly executed.

Jab, rock, bend, plant.

Thinking? There were no thoughts. Except one.

Jab, rock, bend, plant.

More of an image than a thought, really.

Jab, rock, bend, plant.

Her face.

Jab, rock, bend, plant.

Today, as soon as he was done with his bundle, he would race home, hit the shower, then drive downtown to Riverview Terraces, where June would be waiting.

Jab, rock, bend, plant.

He wondered where she was at that moment. Driving up I-35 with her dad? Maybe they were already at the condo, unloading their stuff.

Jab, rock, bend, plant.

Was she thinking about him?

June carried the last suitcase from the back of her Dad's SUV, into the building, up the elevator to the seventeenth floor, down the short hallway to number 170, a completely furnished luxury condo, her home for the next six weeks. Wes would be knocked out by the view, looking out over the river in one direction and downtown in the other.

She plunked the suitcase down in the entryway and flopped down on the long leather sofa.

"June!" Dad was calling from his bedroom. June groaned and got up and went to see what he wanted. He had changed into a suit and was looking in the mirror, tying his tie. "Where's my carry-on?"

June pointed. She had set it at the foot of his bed.

"Oh. Thanks." He snugged up the knot in his tie, lifted the bag onto the bed, and opened it. "Cuff links," he said, digging into one of the many small compartments. June helped him fasten the cuff links. Just like her mother would have.

"Will you be home for dinner?" she asked.

"I'm afraid not, Junie. Business dinner with my new associates. You'll have to fend for yourself." He saw something in June's face. "I imagine you'll be seeing Wes."

"Is it okay if he comes over?"

He looked at her for a long time. June felt herself blushing, though she wasn't sure why.

"I'll be home by nine," he said.

"Okay."

"You start work in the morning."

"Okay."

"We'll go shopping for food tomorrow. Tonight you can order in." He opened his wallet and handed her two twenties. "Pizza, or whatever you want."

"Thanks."

Again, the long, searching look, then he looked at his watch. "I have to go. Call Mom and tell her we've arrived safely. And say hello to Wes for me. Tell him I look forward to spending some time with him. Just the three of us, hanging out."

"Uh, sure, he'd like that." It was all June could do to keep her face blank.

Wes's hair was still wet from the shower when he arrived at Riverview Terraces. He felt strangely cavernous, as if his insides were hollow. He hoped he was dressed okay. He'd changed his shirt three times, finally deciding on the plaid cotton shirt he'd worn the first day he met her. Was that okay? Would she notice?

He stepped out of the elevator on the seventeenth floor. June, wearing jeans and a powder blue T-shirt, stood at the end of the thickly carpeted hallway. Her hair was tied back in a ponytail and her feet were bare. Wes floated toward her. He could not feel his legs. Neither of them spoke.

He was close enough to touch her when she turned and glided into the apartment. He followed her. She led him into a large, high-ceilinged room with tall windows and black leather furniture. They stood in front of the windows, inches between them, and looked out over the river.

Wes's hand found hers. "I can't believe you're here," he said. They weren't looking at each other. Her hand was cool and slightly moist.

"Me neither." She withdrew her hand, turned toward him, and slipped her arms around his back. He did the same. They held each other loosely, not hugging, the fronts of their bodies barely touching. Wes's cheek brushed delicately against her temple. His hands were shivering. He felt her shoulder blade beneath his right thumb; the fingers of his left hand grazed the knobs of her spine. If he squeezed her, would she dissolve like a dream?

June was terrified and she didn't understand why. Who was this boy? What was she doing here, high above the city, alone with him, her breasts separated from his flesh by only three layers of cotton fabric: her bra, her T-shirt, and his plaid flannel? He smelled like deodorant — one of those harsh-smelling brands that boys thought made them smell manly. She wondered what she smelled like. Her shampoo, probably — rosemary — with a whiff of fear sweat and a hint of candy smell from the mint she'd eaten a few minutes earlier. Why was she so jangly?

Wes's arms tightened, just a little. June made her arms do the same, and as she did so, she became acutely aware of her body. She gasped.

Abruptly, Wes released her.

"Are you okay?" he asked.

June nodded, taking a step back. "I just . . . I don't know. This all feels so weird."

"Me too."

"It's like you're not real."

Wes nodded. "I think I've been thinking about seeing you so much that it's like . . . like what if none of this was real? Like we're in a dream or something."

"Maybe we are."

"I wonder if it's your dream or mine."

"I'm pretty sure it's mine."

"Or both of ours. You're still in Omaha, and we're both asleep and our dreams got hooked up."

June felt herself smile, and some of the tension drained from her shoulders. "If it's a dream, we should be able to look out the window and see the Eiffel Tower."

They turned back to the window.

"Doesn't look like Paris," Wes said.

"Dreams are weird."

Wes laughed, and at the sound of his laugh, something inside her came unstuck and she laughed too.

"Do you ever eat pizza in your dreams?" she asked.

"I only dream about two things. Pizza and you."

"In that order?"

"Not always."

"Because I was going to order a pizza. Are you hungry?"

Wes smiled, a wide, open smile that echoed in her heart.

"Always," he said.

FORTY-SIX

Wes was dreaming of trees — pink, pale blue, yellow, lavender, bright orange — all the colors of the rainbow. Except green. He didn't understand how they had changed color, or how he was supposed to plant them. One row of all pink? Or alternate the colors: red, orange, yellow . . . He tried to ask Chuckles what to do, but Chuckles only laughed and laughed and —

Suddenly, he was awake. He felt June's arm draped across his chest, heard her breathing in his ear. He opened his eyes to find Elton Edberg standing over him.

Wes threw June's arm off him and leapt from the sofa. June, startled, let out a yelp and sat up.

"Dad!"

"Hi, honey," said Mr. Edberg, his voice weirdly normal.

Wes's brain creaked and jangled as he strained to throw off the effects of sleep.

"Hi, Mr. Edberg," he said in a muddled voice.

"Hello, Wes. Sleeping with my daughter, I see."

"Daddy! We weren't *doing* anything!"

Mr. Edberg looked at his watch. "Nine o'clock," he said, looking from June to Wes. "Time to leave, don't you think, Wes?"

"Yes, sir," said Wes.

"Unless, of course, you had planned to stay the night?"

"*Daddy!*"

Wes wasn't sure he could move; his feet felt as if they were glued to the carpet. His thoughts flashed back over the evening — the talking, the pizza, more talking, making out . . . of course, Mr. Edberg would know, all he had to do was look at June, at her swollen lips, at the way he had found them wrapped in each other's arms. Was that bad? All he knew was that he was horribly embarrassed. But it wasn't as if he had caught them romping around naked. They'd never even *gotten* naked.

June stood up and took his hand. "Come on. Daddy is just being sadistic and weird."

Elton Edberg's eyebrows lifted. "I'm your father. It's my job."

June rolled her eyes and led Wes to the door. "I'll walk you out."

On the way down, in the elevator, she said, "I don't know why he has to be that way."

"Like he said, it's his job."

"He doesn't have to be so sarcastic."

"Better than chasing me out with a shotgun."

"Daddy doesn't even own a shotgun."

"Probably a good thing."

June rode back up the elevator feeling embarrassed, relieved, and happy: embarrassed because her dad had to be so, well, *embarrassing*. Relieved that he hadn't been as embarrassing as he might have been. And happy because . . . well, not really *happy*, but more like *proud* that her dad had seen her and Wes together that way. Like he had seen that grown-up side of her, more woman than girl. And he hadn't freaked. At least not too badly.

She was pretty sure she hadn't violated any of her mother's rules. Technically.

Back in the condo, her dad was taking a shower. June cleaned up the pizza box, napkins, and glasses she and Wes had dirtied. She plumped and arranged the sofa pillows and set up the coffee machine for the morning. She was wiping down the kitchen counter when her dad came in wearing his bathrobe. He put his hands on her shoulders, looked into her face, kissed her forehead, then went off to bed.

A little later, she called Wes.

"Did you know you're a good kisser?" she said when he answered.

"I am?"

"Yeah. Really good."

"What's good about it?"

"Not too sloppy, not too dry, not too hard, not too, uh, tentative."

"Not tentative? I should put that on my gravestone. *He was not a tentative kisser.*"

"And *hot*. Be sure to add *hot*."

"Are we having phone sex?" he asked.

"You know, my mom forgot to put that on her list of no-nos."

"Everything okay with your dad?"

"Yeah. Dad's fine. We're all good. I start my job tomorrow, putting Humpty Dumpty back together."

They talked for an hour, jumping from one thing to another, until the spaces between their words grew languid and long, and June's eyelids kept falling shut. She didn't remember saying good night, but she must have, because when she woke up at three A.M., her heart pounding from an already-forgotten dream, her phone was perched silently upon her bedside table and all the lights were off. She lay awake for a long time trying to remember her dream, but it would not come.

FORTY-SEVEN

OPERATIONS MANAGER GRETCHEN HILLER, a pinch-faced, dark-haired woman wearing a navy blue suit and high heels, greeted June with a flat smile. "Welcome to my nightmare," she said. She led June to an elevator, heels clicking the marble floor with metronome precision. "Before you ask," she said as they entered the elevator, "this catastrophe was *not* my fault."

"I didn't think that," June said.

Gretchen Hiller compressed her lips and pressed a button labeled *M*.

"Mezzanine?" June guessed, hoping to impress her new boss with her alertness and powers of deduction.

Gretchen Hiller snorted. The elevator began to descend. "Hardly. If it stands for anything, it stands for Most Deep. The room you'll be working in is six levels below street level."

"Oh. No windows?"

The woman gave her a narrow-eyed look. "Go to school for six years, work hard, and get yourself a sex change. *Then* maybe you get a window."

Bitter much? said Sarcastic June — thankfully, not out loud.

The elevator eased to a stop; the doors opened. They were looking directly into a cavernous, white-walled room set up with about twenty long tables arranged end to end in five rows. Nine women of various ages sat at the tables. In front of each of them were several boxes. The boxes were labeled with the names of colors: blue, yellow, pink, lavender, etc. Each woman had a pile of shredded paper in front of her; they were pulling strips of paper from the pile one by one, and putting each one into its appropriate box.

At the far end of the room was a pile of bulging black plastic garbage bags.

"As you can see," said Gretchen Hiller, "the process is both tedious and exacting. We begin by separating the check shreds by color. That will be the easy part. . . ."

By mid-morning, June had learned the names of all the other women. She was the youngest by several years. When they broke for lunch — catered sandwiches that they ate at their work stations — she learned that she had nothing in common with any of them. By two P.M., the only thing keeping June awake was a painful twinge in her lower back and the stinging dryness of her eyes. The tiny strips of paper seemed to suck every molecule of moisture out of the room. Out of her fingers too. At two thirty, Gretchen Hiller came down to check their progress.

She was not pleased.

"At this rate, ladies, we'll be stuck down here until Christmas."

Not me, June said to herself. She would have quit on the spot if it weren't for Wes.

"Maybe if we had some, you know, *ergonomic* chairs it would go faster," she suggested.

Gretchen Hiller gave June a withering look. "You remember what I said about windows?"

June nodded.

"Same goes for ergonomic chairs." She wheeled and clicked back to the elevator. The moment the doors closed, one of the older temps said, "Heil Hitler."

June looked at her, startled.

"Wretched Hitler," the woman explained. "It suits her better than Gretchen Hiller."

They returned to their work.

Wes's phone buzzed as he was starting down his last row for the day.

"Hey."

"Hey. You still working?"

"Yeah, I got about a hundred more trees to plant, then I can go."

"I just got done," June said. "I close my eyes and see little strips of colored paper, mounds of them. One of the women I work with figured out how many we have to sort through. Like five million."

Wes said, "I bet we have the two most boring jobs in the world."

"My boss's nickname is Hitler."

"Mine's Chuckles."

"It's like we're slaves."

"Yeah, exactly. Except for no whipping or chains. And we get paid, and we can quit and go home if we really want to."

"Minor details. Can you come over tonight? Daddy wants the three of us to have dinner. I think he feels bad about scaring you off last night. I'm making chicken."

"Absolutely."

After that, the planting seemed to go a lot faster.

Two hours later, June answered the door wearing an apron and pressing a phone to her ear. *My mom,* she mouthed.

Wes followed her into the kitchen. June was saying, "Uh-huh. Uh-huh. Do I have to stick my hand in there? Yuck."

A whole raw chicken was sitting on the counter, looking pale, flabby, and morose.

June fiddled with the knobs on the oven. "Four hundred? Okay. What if I don't have a meat thermometer? Oh. Okay. So then I just stick it in the oven? Okay. Bye. I'll call you if the kitchen catches fire." She clicked off. "Do you know anything about chickens?" she asked Wes.

"Yeah. They come fried, in cardboard buckets."

"I'm roasting this one. I think."

Wes put his arm around her and they stood together, regarding the chicken.

"I think my mom buys them already cut up," Wes said.

"That's what I should've done. Now I have to put my hand in and pull out the giblets."

"You want me to do it?"

"Yes, please."

"You sure it's dead?" Wes asked.

"Pretty sure."

Wes peered into the chicken. He reached into the cold cavity and pulled out the heart, liver, and gizzard. "Like that?"

"I think so."

"Now what?"

"We salt and pepper it, put it in a big pan with some potatoes and onions, then roast it."

"That's it?"

"According to my mom."

"Why are you making chicken?"

"It's my dad's fave. I was thinking I'd surprise him."

"Oh." Wes had been thinking it was for him. He looked at the pile of slimy organs in his hand. "So what do I do with these?"

With the chicken in the oven, they quickly cleaned up the mess they'd made. Working together in the kitchen was fun — June loved the way they kept bumping into each other, getting in each other's way. Wes kept saying "Sorry" and " 'Scuse me." But she could tell he was bumping her on purpose. She could tell he wanted her, and that made her want him even more.

The next time he bumped her, she threw her sponge in the sink, took off her apron, grabbed his hand, and pulled him into the living room.

"What?" he said.

She kissed him — harder than she ever had before — and pulled him down onto the sofa. The kiss went on until they broke apart, gasping. Wes's eyes had glazed over and his hands were shaking. He made an animal sound, somewhere between a whimper and a growl. She put her fingers to his lips.

"How long?" she said.

Wes's eyes came into focus, a silent question.

She said, "How long do you think it will be before we actually do it?"

"It?"

"Make love for real. Have sex."

Wes swallowed. "Thirty seconds?"

June laughed. "Silly. My dad could walk in anytime." She sat up and ran her fingers through her hair. "Seriously. How long?"

"How long do you want?"

"Part of me wants to do it right now, and part of me wants never."

"Never?"

"So we always have something to look forward to. Like, anticipation is ninety percent of the fun."

"Ninety percent?"

"Give or take. Also, I did sort of promise my mom."

"Oh yeah — the rules."

"The rules."

Wes scrunched up his nose. At first, June thought he was going to say something nasty about her mom, but instead he said, "Do you smell something burning?"

Elton Edberg arrived home to find the condo reeking of smoke, and all the windows wide open. June was in the kitchen scrubbing a blackened roasting pan.

"Junie?" he said.

"Hi, Daddy." She kept on scrubbing.

"What happened?"

"Just a little cooking disaster. I put the oven on broil instead of bake."

"Oh. Is Wes here? I thought the three of us were having dinner together."

The doorbell chimed.

"That's probably him now," June said.

A minute later, Wes came in carrying a red and white bucket of fried chicken with all the fixin's.

FORTY-EIGHT

STANDING ON THE OLD STONE ARCH BRIDGE, June looked down at the brown waters of the Mississippi River. Slow swirls of foam, floating leaves, and bits of trash rode the current, flowing from the north, disappearing beneath the bridge.

"All the way to the Gulf of Mexico," she said.

Wes said, "We could take a boat. Or a raft, like Huck Finn."

During the two weeks June had been in Minneapolis, they had spent every evening together. They had gone for long walks, seen a movie, tried some of the nearby restaurants, and visited a museum. Just the two of them, mostly — except for the time they'd eaten KFC with her dad. They didn't see any of their friends at all. June hadn't even told Britt, Jess, or Phoebe that she was in town. The only person she was interested in was Wes.

"I should probably get back," June said. "Dad's going to be home at six."

"Where's he taking you?"

"Some fancy restaurant. He says we're celebrating."

"Celebrating what?"

"I don't know. He's being very mysterious."

"Maybe he's going to tell you you're not really his daughter. You're the secret love child of a powerful wizard, and you have

superpowers. With a single gesture, you can make all those shredded checks put themselves back together. Or go back in time and
save them from the evil shredder monster."

June laughed. "Do you have any idea how silly you are?"

"I know exactly how silly I am," Wes said with a grin.

"You're still invited, you know."

"I'm still recovering from the last dinner with him. Anyway,
my mom's been giving me grief about never having dinner at home
anymore."

They walked back to June's building without talking. June
kept thinking of things to say, but the silence between them was
too comfortable to break.

The silent times — the two of them together, without talking —
had been getting longer the last few days. Was that okay? Was she
boring when she didn't talk? Did she talk too much? Maybe
she should be more mysterious. Maybe he'd gotten to know her
too well, and now she wasn't interesting anymore. Was it possible to get to know someone too well? Was it possible she could lose
interest in him? She looked at him out of the corner of her eye.
What was he thinking right now?

She had no idea. Once, after some boys had teased her at
school — she had been about thirteen — she had asked her mom,
"What's wrong with boys, anyway? What are they *thinking*?"

"Boys only think about one thing," her mother had
said. "Sex."

But Wes wasn't like that. He thought about all kinds of things.
But he had to think about sex sometimes. Maybe even as much as
she did.

"What are you thinking about?" she asked him.

"Huh?"

"What were you thinking about. Two seconds ago?"

"Oh. Um . . . I was thinking about what my mom was going to make for dinner. Why?"

"Never mind," she said.

Food would have been her second guess.

What Wes was thinking about — he would never have admitted this to June — was how nice it would be to go home and shower and eat with his sister and his parents, and watch some TV without having to talk about what he was watching, and then go to bed early. Because even though June was the most important person in the universe and spending time with her was, mostly, all he wanted to do . . . it wore him out sometimes.

And he was thinking about last week's fried chicken dinner with Elton Edberg, how Mr. Edberg had asked him a thousand questions: *Where do you plan to go to college? What do you want to do with your life? Have you considered banking? Have you considered the military? Who do you plan to vote for in the next election? It's not too soon to open an IRA account. Do you go to church? What does your father do?*

Most of the questions had been about things Wes had never thought much about. By the end of the evening, his brain had been in complete overload.

He kissed June good-bye in front of her building, then walked down the block to where he'd parked. As he got closer to the car, the tension flowed out of his neck and shoulders. *Being in love is hard*, he thought — wanting to be perfect for her every second they were together, and trying not to think too much about the scary, murky future when they would be apart. Between the tree planting and his time with June, he was exhausted.

He had never been happier in his life.

FORTY-NINE

JUNE'S DAD TALKED ON HIS CELL from the time they left the condo until they got to the restaurant. Watching him in action — switching from call to call, changing tone from demanding to cajoling to syrupy sweet depending on what he wanted from whoever he was talking to — was both impressive and sickening. June considered taking out her own cell and calling Wes. Just to make a point. But she didn't.

Her dad didn't stop with his phone calling until they were seated in the restaurant, then he made a big show of turning his phone off.

"Isn't this nice?" he said.

June wasn't sure if he was referring to the two of them being together, or to having turned off his cell phone, or to the restaurant itself.

"It's sure *big*," she said, going with the third option. Everything at Sammy's Steak House was huge: high ceilings, oversize water glasses and utensils, towel-size napkins. . . . Even the leather-bound menus were enormous. She looked around at the other customers. They were big too. Probably from eating at Sammy's.

"*Big* is Sammy's claim to fame. The biggest and the best. I hope you're hungry."

The menu, as big as it was, had limited choices: six types of steak on the left side, with pork chops, lamb chops, scallops, and whole lobster on the right. June decided on the scallops. They would be the easiest to eat. Her dad ordered a rib eye steak.

While they waited for their food, he asked her how work was going.

"Incredibly boring," June said. "It's going to take at least another month. Maybe longer. Wretched Hitler is getting more perturbed every day."

"Wretched Hitler?"

"I mean Gretchen Hiller. Some of the women call her Wretched Hitler. Not to her face, of course."

Elton Edberg grinned. "I wonder what my employees call me."

"The Terminator," June said.

"Really?" He frowned slightly, then shrugged. "That's not so bad. At least it shows that I have their respect."

"I was kidding," June said.

"Oh?" he said, not at all embarrassed. "You have your mother's sense of humor."

"Mom has a sense of humor?"

"Oh yes. She keeps me on my toes. I imagine you do the same with Wes. How are you two doing?"

"Fine," said June.

"That's it? Just 'fine'?"

June nodded. Her father frowned.

The awkward moment was interrupted by the arrival of their meals. June's sea scallops were the size of hockey pucks. Her dad's rib eye steak was almost four inches thick.

"Look at this potato!" her dad said.

"Are you sure that's not a loaf of bread?" June said.

He stabbed the potato with his knife. "Nope. Potato."

The outsize portions made her dad feel important, but for June, everything about the place made her feel small.

"So what are we celebrating?" June asked as she cut into a giant scallop with her giant knife.

"Oh, *that*!" he said as if it had entirely slipped his mind. "Benford Bank has offered me a full-time position."

"Here?" June didn't even try to keep the hope and desperation out of her voice.

"Well . . . for the next month, at least. Actually, there are several possibilities — Omaha, Des Moines, Fargo . . ." He cut a large piece of steak, put it in his mouth, and chewed. June had been taught to not ask questions of people who were in the process of chewing, but this was too much.

"Fargo?"

He started to answer, hesitated, then made an effort to swallow, opened his mouth . . . and froze. For a moment, June thought he was making a funny face, though she couldn't imagine why. Then his eyes went big and round and he clutched his throat; the skin around his eyes turned red, veins bulged, his mouth opened and closed soundlessly.

June heard herself scream.

"Be still my heart!" Wes's mom put her hands to her chest. "Is my son going to consent to joining us for dinner?"

Wes rolled his eyes. His mom smirked and stirred something on the stove.

"We hardly see you anymore," she said.

"That's because I work ten hours a day. Also, June's only going to be here for a few weeks, so, you know . . ."

"Is everything all right with you two?" his mom asked.

"Yeah. Her dad is taking her to a restaurant tonight."

"It's good to take a break sometimes. Will we ever get to meet her?"

"Uh . . ."

"Yeah!" Paula materialized in the doorway. "I want to know what she looks like."

"Why don't you bring her by for dinner tomorrow night?" his mom said.

"I bet she's really pretty," said Paula.

"Uh . . . I could ask her."

"Or maybe she's ugly," Paula said.

"She is *not* ugly!"

"We could do steaks on the grill. Everybody likes steak."

"Daddy!"

He was trying to stand up, one hand clutching his throat, the other waving desperately in the air. June could sense movement, every head in the restaurant turning toward their table. A man — their waiter — appeared behind her father and wrapped his arms around him. She heard a grunt of effort, then a wet, popping sound, and something hit her on the chest.

Her father drew a ragged breath. The waiter released him; her father slumped back into his chair. June looked down at the half-chewed hunk of steak rolling down the front of her white top, and she realized what had just happened. Her father had been choking.

"Thank you," he gasped, looking up at the waiter.

"Not a problem, sir. The Heimlich maneuver is a part of our training."

"Yes, well, you have been very well trained."

"Thank you, sir. Enjoy the rest of your meal."

June used her napkin to pick the hunk of masticated meat from her lap.

"Excuse me," she said. She dropped the napkin on the floor and walked quickly through the restaurant to the restroom, where she did her best to wipe the stain from her top. She was able to get most of it out, but the wet spot between her breasts was obvious. Leaning over the hand dryer, holding out the front of her top to blast it with hot air — what had just happened hit her with full force.

He had almost died. If it had happened at home, with no one else around, she would have stood by helplessly as he choked to death. A whirlpool formed inside her chest, threatening to suck her insides out; she let out a gasp, squeezed her eyes shut, and sank to her knees on the restroom floor.

"Are you all right?" asked a woman's voice.

June forced herself to breathe, to open her eyes. A woman in a waiter's uniform was bending over her. June managed a weak smile.

"I'm fine," she said. "It was just a twinge." She stood up shakily and quickly left the restroom.

Her father had finished most of his dinner. He smiled and asked if she was okay.

"I'm fine," she said. A fresh napkin had been laid next to her plate.

"You were gone a long time. I sent one of the waitresses in to check on you."

"I was trying to clean my shirt."

"Oh. Well, it looks fine! Dig in!" He went right back to his rib eye, eating with as much gusto as before, but taking smaller bites.

June was careful not to ask any questions while her dad was chewing. In fact, she was terrified to do or say anything. Her appetite was gone. All she could do was watch her dad shovel food into his mouth.

Noticing that June wasn't eating, he set down his knife and fork.

"I've spoiled your appetite, haven't I?"

"You almost *died*!" she said.

"But I didn't."

June glared at him. "You would have if that waiter hadn't done that Heimlich thing."

"I'm sure if he hadn't, you would have. Don't they teach the Heimlich maneuver in school?"

"Not in any school *I've* been to. Besides, I thought you were having a heart attack."

He shrugged and said, "Oh, well. Life is just one near-death experience after another."

"Is that going to be another one of your sayings?"

He gave her his patented Elton Edberg smile. "Do you like it?"

Wes said, "He's okay, isn't he?"

"That's not the point."

"So what *is* the point?"

"The *point* is, he almost *died*!"

"Yeah, well, he didn't." Wes was feeling irritable. He thought he might be experiencing withdrawal symptoms, like he'd gotten addicted to spending several hours a day with June. Talking on the phone only heightened his frustration.

June said, "But he *could* have. It could happen to anybody, anytime. So what's the use?"

"The use of what?"

"Of everything!"

Wes couldn't tell if she was really asking him that, or just trying to confuse him.

"I guess we just have to have fun while we're still alive," he said.

"All you think about is having fun. And eating."

Huh? Where did *that* come from? Wes didn't know what to say, so he waited for June to continue.

She said, "I mean, what are we *doing*, anyway?"

"Talking on the phone?"

June didn't say anything for a second; Wes was afraid she was going to hang up on him again.

"Why don't you come over?" she said. "Right now."

"Now? It's almost ten!"

"So?"

"They'd never let me use the car this late."

"You're not coming over?"

"I don't think I should."

"Thanks a lot!"

June knew she was being a whiny bitch again, making him feel bad when he hadn't done anything wrong. Why did she want him to come over anyway? He was right — the minute he got there, it would be time for him to go home. It was just stupid. But she hated that he wouldn't do it.

Wes said, "Look, if you really want me to, I'll take a bus downtown."

"My dad would just tell you to go home."

"That's what I'm saying!"

June closed her eyes and swallowed.

"June?"

"What."

"Do you want me to come over?"

"Yes. No. No, it would be stupid."

She heard him exhale, probably with relief.

"My mom wants you to come over for dinner tomorrow," he said.

"To your house?"

"They want to meet you."

"Why?"

"My sister wants to know if you're as beautiful as I think you are."

"Oh!" He thought she was beautiful? June looked in the mirror. No way.

"June? Are you there?"

"I'm here."

After Wes said good night to June, he went downstairs. His parents were on the sofa, watching a talk show. Paula was sitting in the recliner, reading.

"June says she can come for dinner tomorrow," he told his mom.

"That's wonderful," she said.

"Who's coming to dinner?" his dad asked.

"Wes's *girlfriend*," said Paula. "They're in *love*."

Wes rolled his eyes. His mom laughed. His dad went back to watching TV.

"Do you think we could have something besides steak?" Wes said.

"Is she vegetarian?"

"No, it's just . . . she has this problem with steak." He thought for a moment, then added, "We probably shouldn't have roast chicken, either."

CHAPTER FIFTY

JUNE OPENED A CAN OF TOMATO SOUP, dumped it in a pan, and put it on the stove. She sliced cheddar cheese and made a sandwich — lots of butter on the outside — and put it in a frying pan. She tore open a bag of prewashed salad greens, put them in a wooden bowl, and put it on the table with a bottle of ranch dressing. She set the table for one.

All her dad had to do was turn on the burners, and in about five minutes he would be eating. Grilled cheese sandwich and tomato soup — the ultimate comfort food, and hard to choke on. The salad was because she'd promised her mom to make sure he ate something green with every meal.

She frowned at the table she had set. Her mom would have put out candles, or a floral centerpiece. June shrugged; she was not her mother. Besides, Wes would be picking her up in about twenty minutes. Time to start working on her face. She wanted to make a good impression.

Wes said, "Wow."

June smiled.

Wes said, "You look . . . really different."

June's smile quivered and began to fade.

Wes said, "Good! I mean, you look great."

"Too much makeup?" she asked. She might have gone overboard on the eye shadow.

"No! I mean, I've just never seen you so, uh, glamorous."

"Is glamorous okay?"

"Yeah! I mean, you look fine."

He was lying. She felt a little sick. His parents would hate her.

"I'll go back upstairs and wash it off."

"No! We don't want to be late. My mom has a thing about that." He took her hand and coaxed her into the car. "Besides, they don't care what you look like."

On the drive over to Wes's house, June could feel her insides crumbling. She knew she had on too much makeup. It was supposed to make her confident and safe, like wearing a mask, but suddenly she was feeling like a clown. A slutty clown. She pulled down the visor and regarded herself in the tiny mirror. Wes was watching her out of the corner of his eye. She took a tissue from her purse and began wiping away some of the eye shadow. Of course, it smeared. She worked on it all the way there. By the time they pulled into his driveway, she had succeeded in making both eyes look the same: like a sad raccoon.

"How do I look now?" she asked.

"You look beautiful," Wes said. He leaned over and kissed her on the cheek.

June examined her reflection. "Yeah, like I haven't slept in a week."

Paula was standing in the entryway waiting for them. Her enormous eyes locked on June like twin lasers. When she opened her mouth to speak, Wes braced himself, certain that something embarrassing was about to come out.

Paula said, "Hi."

"You must be Paula," June said. Wes could tell she was nervous, biting her lip, messing up her lipstick.

"You're prettier than I thought," Paula said.

June tipped her head. "What did you think I'd look like?"

"No offense, but my brother normally doesn't have very good taste."

Wes faked a slap at the top of Paula's head; Paula ducked, laughing. June was smiling — that was good.

Their mom's voice came from the kitchen, "Are they here?"

"Yes!" Paula yelled.

"Come on," Wes said. "Let's meet the rest of the zoo."

June had been prepared for the sort of grilling her dad had put Wes through, but the Andrews family wasn't like that. Wes's mom was friendly and nice, and her questions were easy ones — *How do you like living downtown? I hear you have a very unusual job! Do you like lasagna?* — nothing about the future, nothing she couldn't answer. Mr. Andrews, who looked like a thicker, older version of Wes, was nice too. He didn't say much, just a few remarks, like asking her what her dad did, and telling her that Benford Bank was "a fine company, very respected." Paula was the chattiest one in the family, and the most interesting because anything might come out of her mouth at any time.

As they were sitting down to dinner, Paula said, "Can you show me how to do makeup?" That was a little embarrassing because it make everybody look at her face at the same time.

"Um . . . I don't really wear makeup, usually," June said.

"You're wearing makeup now."

"I was sort of experimenting."

"It looks cool."

June caught Mrs. Andrews's eye. She was smiling, but not in a nasty way — more like she completely understood and was amused not by June's makeup disaster, but by Paula's kidlike directness.

"You're twelve, right?" June added two years to Paula's real age.

"Ten!"

"Really?"

"I should know how old I am."

"Tell you what, when you turn thirteen, I'll give you a makeup lesson, if you still want it."

"That's a long time. What if you're not still Wes's girlfriend?"

The strangest thing happened then: Everybody laughed. Even Paula. Even June.

When they got in the car so Wes could drive June home, she didn't say anything for the first few blocks. Finally, as they were pulling onto the freeway, Wes asked her what she thought about his family.

She said, "It's what I want."

"What is?"

"I want a family like yours. That's what I want. In a real house that you live in for years and years, and everybody likes each other, and they laugh at stuff, and nobody gets mad."

"They get mad." He turned onto the freeway. "They were pretty mad when they had to come get me out of jail in Omaha."

"Your mom's really nice."

"You have a nice mom too."

"Yeah, but it's different. We move around so much. My dad's wound up all the time, worrying about work and stuff, and my mom gets all frantic trying to be the good wife. We can't ever just relax and be who we really are with each other. We don't laugh."

"Your dad laughs."

"That's different. He laughs when he thinks he's scored a point, or when he's trying to cover up being embarrassed or anxious."

"He gets anxious?"

"Sometimes I think he's scared all the time. It makes me scared too."

"Scared of what?"

"For one thing, I'm scared that I'll go upstairs and find out he choked."

Elton Edberg was alive, sitting in the black leather recliner, watching TV.

"Wes!" he boomed.

"Hi, Mr. E." Since Wes had never gotten comfortable calling Mr. Edberg "El," they had compromised at "Mr. E."

"How was your date?"

June said, "It wasn't really a date, Daddy. We went to Wes's house for dinner."

"Of course! To meet the outlaws." He laughed.

"Outlaws?"

"You know — if you two were married, Wes's folks would be your *in-laws*." He laughed again, and Wes could see what June had been talking about: That was a point-scoring laugh.

June said, "I was worried you might have choked on your grilled cheese."

"*Grilled?* I was supposed to *cook* it?"

"Why did you think I left it sitting in a pan?"

"Oh!" He laughed again, a covering-up-embarrassment laugh. "I guess that explains why the bread was buttered on the outside."

June was looking at the TV. "What are you watching, Daddy?"

"Oh, just some old thing."

It was a black-and-white movie. Wes recognized Humphrey Bogart.

"Is it *Casablanca*?" he asked.

"Very good, Wes! It was my parents' favorite movie."

"Since when do you watch anything except the business channel?" June said.

"It's a good movie. Why don't you two sit down and watch it with me?"

Driving home, Wes couldn't stop thinking about the movie. They'd only watched the last forty minutes — the most he'd watched of any black-and-white movie, ever — so everything that happened didn't make complete sense, but he got the gist of it: Humphrey Bogart giving up the girl because he knew it was the right thing to do. During the last scene, as Bogart watched his one true love walk out of his life forever, Wes had looked at Mr. Edberg and could have sworn he saw tears in his eyes. It was embarrassing, but it made Wes like him better.

Then he started wondering if Mr. Edberg had made them sit and watch the movie to make a point. That June would be better off without him. But he was pretty sure those tears had been real.

FIFTY-ONE

ONCE ALL THE SHREDDED CHECK COLORS had been separated into bins, the women began dividing the strips according to check pattern. The process was slow and exacting. It was August by the time the work of piecing together each individual check began. The first time she assembled one entire check, June's boredom turned to elation. One down, five thousand nine hundred ninety-nine to go. The other temps were having success as well. With each reassembled check, the piles of strips grew smaller, and the job slowly moved toward completion. Some of the women deliberately slowed down. They needed the work, and the sooner the temp job was done, the sooner they would have to look for another source of income.

June slowed down as well. Whether the job was done or not, she would be flying back to Omaha before school started. She tried to talk her mom into letting her stay with Dad, but there was no way.

"I am not spending another month in this house all by myself!" her mom said.

"You could move up here."

"Junie, that's not how it works."

"Because it's not how you *want* it to work!"

Her mom sighed so loudly it sounded as if she was blowing into the phone. "Honey, I know that you and Wes are really serious.

But if you're as in love as you think you are, a little time apart won't hurt. It might actually be good."

"Good for who?"

"For everybody," her mom said in a barely audible voice.

When she got all soft and quiet like that, June knew it was time to stop fighting. Besides, she knew her mom was right. She and Wes had been together almost every single day for weeks. She knew his face better than she knew her own. She could close her eyes and feel his lips on hers, almost as if he were really there. They had become so close that the idea of being apart didn't frighten her anymore, because even when she wasn't with him, he was a part of her.

They settled into a routine. Wes would rush home from his planting job, shower, and either borrow his mom's car or take a bus downtown. If the weather was nice, they would go for a long walk along the river. If it was rainy or too hot, they would hang out at the condo, watching TV or just talking, until Mr. E got home, usually around seven.

Sometimes Wes would help her make dinner. Even though he was hopelessly clumsy in the kitchen, it was always fun. June knew how to make about ten different things: grilled cheese, scrambled eggs, hamburgers, spaghetti, tuna casserole — things like that — but she never tried to roast another chicken.

At home, as long as he was home by ten every night, his parents mostly left him alone, not quizzing him too much about what was going on with him and June. Every now and then, he caught his mother giving him this sad look. Paula was getting older every day, pointedly ignoring him as she immersed herself in phone calls and online girl chat. It was almost as if he was leaving them all behind. He would be a senior in a few weeks, and after that would come college and a new life. He was holding off on choosing a school, waiting to find out where June might be going. It was one of the things they hadn't really talked about.

They decided that one day a week they would go a whole twenty-four hours without seeing each other, just to prove they could do it. Wes would hook up with Calvin or Robbie after work and play video games or whatever. At first, when he was with his friends, it felt unreal — as if June was his real life, and his old friends were synthetic. But after a few hours, the feeling reversed, and June became the fantasy.

He and Calvin were in the arcade at the mall one evening when Wes saw June walk past. He started after her, then hung back to see where she was going. Abercrombie & Fitch. She took some tops into the dressing room. Wes stood behind a display at the back of the store and imagined her changing clothes. It felt strange being so close to her without her knowing, but also exciting, just knowing she was there. After several minutes, she came out and returned the tops to their racks and left without buying anything.

He followed her to Macy's, where he lost track of her in the maze of counters and displays. He wandered through the store searching for her as if in a dream, everything too bright, too in focus, not real. Had he really seen her, or had he made it up?

After a time, he gave up and returned to the arcade. Calvin, still playing Street Fighter, looked at him and said, "Dude. Are you okay?"

That night, he called June and told her he'd seen her at the mall.

"I saw you," she said.

"You did?"

"At Abercrombie, in a mirror. I pretended I didn't know you were there. When I went in the dressing room, I kept thinking you might come in."

"What, walk into the women's dressing room?"

"It would be a good place to get naked and have sex."

Wes felt all the blood and heat in his body rush south.

June said, "But if we did, I don't think I could ever stand to be without you."

Wes made an inarticulate sound deep in his throat.

They didn't talk about sex much, but it was always there. They would make out, and then when things got really hot, they would always stop, like hitting an invisible wall, leaving Wes feeling as if he'd been punched in the gut, followed by a swirly, bubbly sensation that reminded him of the time he'd climbed a grain elevator, ten stories tall, and forced himself to stand right on the edge.

If they went all the way, it would be over — whatever this thing was that they had going. Like the end of a journey. Or maybe it would be the next stage of another journey.

It wasn't about abstinence, or what was right and what was wrong, or any of that stuff. It was more about finding that perfect moment — a point in time that was sometimes minutes, sometimes hours, sometimes years in the future.

"We'll be done with the checks in a week or two," June said.

"That's great," said Wes, wondering what that had to do with getting naked in the Abercrombie dressing room.

"I have to go home when my job ends."

"Home?"

"To Omaha."

All that blood and heat moved up to his stomach.

"I thought your dad got that job permanently."

"He did, but he's still not sure where they're going to send him. Mom and I will be staying in Omaha. Temporarily. So I have to go back and get ready for school and stuff. Also, I think my mom's lonely."

"Oh." Wes waited for his insides to settle.

"You know what she told me once? She said being apart is part of being in love."

"What does that *mean*?"

"I don't know."

"WHEN DO THE METEORS START?" June asked. They were reclined on the hood of Wes's dad's car, their backs against the windshield.

"I don't think meteors have a schedule," Wes said.

June shifted her body closer, so their shoulders pressed hard together. Above them, the myriad stars pulsed and glittered.

"So many," she said. "So far away."

They stared up into the sky.

"I can see the Milky Way," June said.

"They named it after the candy bar."

"They did not!" She looked at Wes, at his little smile, and kissed him on the corner of his mouth. "You are so goofy."

"Goofy?"

"Goofy."

"That sounds like something Paula would say."

"Smart girl."

They watched the stars.

"Summer is almost over," Wes said.

"At least it's not a thousand degrees out." The previous week had been hot and sticky. Every afternoon, when June left the air-conditioned bank building, it had been like stepping into an oven, but the day before a cold front had rolled in from Canada, and the air had turned dry and crisp. "I'm actually kind of cold."

"I can fix that." Wes rolled off the hood and got a wool blanket from the trunk. He looked around, scanning the horizon from the hilltop where they had parked. There were a few lights in the distance: farms, a handful of red blinking cell tower lights, a subtle glow from the Twin Cities forty miles to the south. Most of the light came from the stars, though. That was the idea, to find a place where the stars could shine.

"You must have been a Boy Scout," June said as they snuggled beneath the scratchy blanket. "Be prepared."

"I think my dad was a Scout. He's the one who told me about the meteor shower. Tonight is supposed to be the peak."

"How many meteors are there?"

"Millions. But only a few thousand you can see."

June was falling up. Gravity had lost its hold; the starry sky was swallowing them. She squeezed Wes's hand, but the sensation persisted.

"It feels like flying," she whispered.

"I know," he said. "If you look up so all you can see is stars, it's like being weightless. Do you know where the center is?"

"Center of what?"

"The universe. The place where the Big Bang started."

"I don't think the universe has a center."

"How can it not have a center?"

"According to Mr. Reinhardt, the universe has no center and no edges."

"It had to start somewhere!"

"When the Big Bang happened, there was no 'somewhere.' There was no time and no space. Just nothing and nowhere. And then it happened, and suddenly there was something and everywhere."

"What about the Big Crunch? That has to happen *sometime* and *someplace*, right? I mean, if everything starts moving together, there has to be a time and place where it will all meet. Right?"

"It will meet everywhere at once. At the end of time."

"It hurts my head to think that," Wes said.

"I like it. I like thinking about things that are far away. It's the in-between stuff that's hard. It's easy to think — to talk — about things that won't happen for a long time. Like living in a real house, or having kids, or the end of the world. The same goes for close stuff — what's going to happen in the next hour, or tomorrow. But the in-between stuff . . ." Her eyes blurred; the stars became streaky and smudged. June spoke under her breath, barely breathing the words, "That's harder."

"You mean in a week or two," Wes said.

"And a month, and two months. The in-between future. Where we'll be. What we'll be doing. I go back to Omaha. You meet a girl —"

"I don't *want* to meet a girl!"

"But maybe you do meet somebody. You can't know for sure. You met me." She squeezed his hand hard. "You didn't plan it — neither of us did — it just happened. It could happen again. You meet a girl and I — I don't know — my dad moves us to Tierra del Fuego or someplace, and I stow away on a cargo ship and come back and you're married with two kids. . . ."

"I don't *want* two kids. I want *you*."

"In the close future, yeah. But the in-between future, you don't know. Neither of us does."

She could hear Wes breathing. Their clasped hands were slippery with perspiration, but her lips were dry. She moistened them with her tongue and said, "I'm just saying that things will change, and it's hard. Except for one thing."

"What's that?" Wes's voice was a croak.

"You will always be the first boy I ever loved. And I will love you forever, even if we are living on opposite sides of the world. Even if someday we hate each other, I will always love you."

"Me too," Wes said, his voice so thick she could hardly understand him. "I love you too."

June sensed something from the corner of her eye. She turned her head just in time to see a bright slash near the horizon. "I saw one!"

"Where?"

"It's gone."

"Did you make a wish?"

"It was too fast."

The meteor shower began slowly. Every minute or so the bright streaks would come and go, leaving blue afterimages in Wes's eyes. As time passed, as the universe expanded, the flashes came more frequently, occasionally several at once, and he gave himself up to the spectacle, anchored only by June's hand, knowing that even if he were to fly from the face of the earth, she would be there, always, until the end of time.

AUTHOR'S NOTE AND ACKNOWLEDGMENTS

My original draft of *The Big Crunch* ended on Valentine's Day, when Wes answers the phone and finds June at the other end. I thought the book was perfect and complete, so I sent the manuscript off to my editor, David Levithan, who responded with an email saying, "I love the book, but the story isn't over yet. I want more. Like, a hundred pages more."

That is most definitely *not* what a writer who thinks he has just finished a novel wants to hear. David can be incredibly aggravating . . . especially when he is right. And he *was* right — Wes and June still had a long journey ahead of them, and so did I. Thank you, David.

My thanks also to the usual suspects — Mary, Kathy, Deborah, and Pat, and to my dental hygienist and plot consultant Lindsey Erickson, and to Kati Oakes, who gently and astutely critiqued an early draft of the manuscript.